BOLTED

SUSAN S. MAIRE

Chapter 1

It started out as an ordinary, wonderful Saturday. I was about to go to the barn and ride. I was already awake, anxious to start the day, by the time I heard my father moving around getting dressed. It was still early, just after 6:30. The sun was up, it looked to be a beautiful day. Little did I know as I dressed how this day would change me and bring challenges to overcome that I had never dreamed would exist.

I smiled as I pulled on my jodhpurs and a polo shirt. Thank goodness! Today, I didn't have to dress in the formal shirt, stock collar, and jacket my mother insisted were proper attire for the country club dining room The barn where I rode horses was on the grounds of the country club where my father was the golf pro. Today I would not be having dinner at the club with my father, as I sometimes did.

Weekends, if I got up early enough, I could go to the club with my father. Unless he came home early, I would pack a sandwich and stuff for lunch, but have dinner at the club with him.

On the drive to the country club I commented to my father "I'm really glad that Mr. DeLong took Patty and me riding that day. I don't think I have ever felt anything so great in my life. My body seemed to naturally become one with the rhythm of the horse's walk. "

As I thought about that first day it suddenly occurred to me to ask, "Did you feel that way when you first played golf?"

"Certainly not at the very beginning. I started out caddying for the members of the neighboring country club. The course was closed on Mondays so they let the caddies play if they wanted to. Those first attempts were pretty wild—lots of windmill swings and slams into the ground. But then there came the moment when everything was right. There was that solid *cr -r- rack* as my driver's sweet spot made solid contact with the ball and it went sailing down the fairway, straight and true. I guess that was when I knew that I wanted to keep sending a ball down fairways like that. There are always plenty of challenges in golf. It's a pretty complex game, different clubs and different kinds of strokes Your long legs would be an asset in golf as well as riding."

"Yeah, but the ball doesn't nicker a hello to you and be glad to see you," I replied. "And besides, I don't have time to do both."

My very best friend Patty DeLong lived next door. Her family had moved into their house the week before we moved into ours. We were the same age and both about to start fourth grade. She immediately became the sister I didn't have. She was lucky, her brother—she had only one— was younger than she was. I had the misfortune to have two of them and they were both older than I. Having a sister, even if not a real one, made-up for having to put up with two older brothers— almost.

We were just starting fifth grade when Patty's father learned that stables had re-opened on the grounds of the country club. He had played polo when he was younger so he thought Patty should try riding.

When he had suggested it, recognizing that neither one of us did anything alone if possible, he had added, "Katlyn, you're welcome to come too, if it's alright with your parents. "

With my father being a professional athlete, my brothers and I had been exposed to a lot of different sports, but never anything to do with horses. My mother had ridden a few times when she was younger but since she wasn't much of an animal person nor sportswoman, it didn't last long. However, she thought riding was a skill that a properly brought up young lady might acquire so she gave permission to join

Patty for the outing. I had always had an affinity for animals so I was really excited to have the chance to get acquainted with horses.

With both trepidation and excitement, we climbed into Mr. DeLong's car and off we went to the stables. Patty was unusually quiet." What's the matter?" I asked.

"I'm not certain this is going to be something I like. In fact, I'm fairly sure I'm not going to like it. I already am scared and we aren't even there yet," she replied. I didn't know what to say to her since I could hardly wait to get there.

The horses were ready when we arrived. Patty looked at me nervously. "I didn't think they would be so big" Although more excited than nervous I had to agree they did look big! We were shown how to mount and hold the reins. Mr. DeLong helped Warren, the manager and head instructor at the barn to lead Patty and me on our first ride. We walked down the drive to the ring. Even though we were only walking, it was wonderful. The sun was brighter, the breeze more pleasant, the air clearer. Everything was just perfect! I was hooked.

Sad to say, Patty's reaction to our first ride was quite different. As soon as her horse began to walk she cried "Slow it down. It's going too fast," then, "Daddy, don't let go of him." For her, being high off the ground was scary. She was so tense she couldn't follow the motion of the horse. She was sure that the gentle school horse was going to turn into a bucking bronc of the West at any moment!

The hour of that first ride flew by much too quickly for me. At the end of it, we had to leave the horses and stable and return to our mundane world at home. I was so-o-o glad my father went to the country club every day. Lucky me. I had ready access to this new fantastic world, without depending on Mr. DeLong. I was so wound-up and excited at the prospect of exploring this wonderful new world, I hardly gave a thought to the fact that Patty wouldn't be sharing it with me. Nor had I given any thought to what my mother's views on the subject might be if I were to continue to be involved with horses.

SUSAN S. MAIRE

The Barn

Chapter 2

We arrived at the club, I left Dad opening the pro shop and headed to the ninth green and fairway. Carefully skirting the green, my boots with heels would surely have left gouges in the green, I took off down the ninth fairway still sparkling with early morning dew. A few yards beyond the gold back tees, I was right in the middle of the outside hunt course, between the picket fence jump and the water jump. I jumped the water jump, just because— it was there, it was Saturday, and I was at the barn.

I was there early enough to help with getting horses ready for the day. As I went about grooming school horses, I planned what my riding buddy, Priscilla (Cilla) and I would do once she got here. I was also hoping that this would be a typical Saturday and there would be people arriving to go on a trail ride. That meant free riding! As luck would have it, shortly before 10:00 o'clock a group of people did arrive.

Warren called to me. "Katlyn, would you get ready and ride with these nice people so they won't get lost?"

"Gladly, "I answered. Turning to one of those standing nearby, I said: "there are over seventy miles of trails so it's easy to get confused as to the way back to the barn." Of course, the real purpose of having someone with them was so they didn't go tearing around like drunk cowboys and injure the horses!

With a smile on my face, I got ready to lead them out. A chance to ride an extra hour without having to pay for it and I was riding "Jim!" He was a boarder's Tennessee Walking horse that I was using to give him some exercise while his owner was away. He was great fun to ride and had very different gaits from the school horses.

The day was turning out to be a lovely day. Blue skies with just a few cotton puff clouds that you could imagine were different animals or something. Enough breeze to make riding a pleasure, but not strong enough to get the horses hyper.

Priscilla (Cilla) had arrived at the barn when I returned from the trail ride. She had started riding with Hazel and Warren who owned the stables when they had their barn in Rowley, where Cilla lived. Even though we didn't go to school together, we spent most weekends at the barn and were close friends. Cilla was a fearless rider, not particularly elegant but she could stay on any horse.

After the trail ride group left and the horses were put away, Warren's wife, Hazel, asked me "Did you see the new sales horse we just brought in? He needs to get out and see his new surroundings. Do you want to take him for a ride? "

"I saw him earlier but I didn't recognize him. I was wondering who he was. Sure, I'd love to try him. Where is his tack and we'll get him ready." I went to his stall and brought him out onto the cross-ties in the aisle. His name was 'Socks' which was to be expected as he had four evenly matched white lower legs. I suppose he could also have been called 'Blaze' since he had a white blaze down his face, but he wasn't. I later learned that he was described as 'having a lot of chrome' which made him very flashy and a horse one notices. That made him a good sale horse for the barn. While Cilla and I put on his saddle and bridle he seemed quite interested in us and what we were doing, but quiet and mannerly.

I mounted and walked down the driveway to the ring. Cilla came down to watch and be my ground person. That included everything from telling me if what I was doing was working to teasing and joking about how badly I rode. Things went well at first. We walked for a bit while I got the feel of him. He had a nice, long, swinging walk. I said to Cilla "He is really fussy about how much contact with his mouth you take." Trotting was a bit fast but then he seemed to settle down a bit.

"Try a canter," called Cilla. That's when we had our first disagreement. I wanted to stop cantering and he didn't. Out the open gate of the arena, and up the drive to the barn we went. "*Well,*" I thought, "*that didn't go very well. But, no big deal. After all, it's my first time on the horse.*" When he did it a second time, I began to be a little concerned. Cilla was giving me a hard time about letting him take me back to the barn not once but twice so it was becoming a challenge to stop him from doing it.

After the second time, Hazel said "Cilla put the bars across the arena gate, and Katlyn, let him see that the bars are up. He's been in arenas before. He'll recognize the gate is closed so it won't happen again." Sounded to me like a good idea that should solve the problem and everything would be OK.

And it appeared to work. Both of us started to get our act together and work things out when suddenly he was airborne, taking off like a rocket, heading right for the arena gate. "*What happened?*". All I could see was that four and one-half foot gate looming up in front of me. I remembered even if he didn't, that the bars were up, a fact that did not appear to concern him at all! Just the thought of trying to jump a four and one-half foot fence was terrifying.

Careening toward the gate at the speed of an express train, I shortened my left rein, trying to turn him before reaching the gate. My single coherent thought (if I had one) was "*if I could get him turned, he could run along the long side of the arena until I could stop him.*" It didn't quite work out the way that way. Either I was too slow or he was too fast. Granted, we didn't jump the gate. And I did manage to turn him somewhat. But not enough to make the curve of the ring, Before I could release the breath I was holding when he didn't jump the gate bars, CA-RA-CK! We crashed through the top rail at the corner of the ring, breaking the post just above the bottom rail. Socks managed to jump over the loosened-but-still-there bottom rail of the fence and I managed to stay on him. Now we were headed right at the first jump of the outside hunt course!

My left rain was frozen in place, still trying to turn him. It did bend him just enough that Socks went to the side of the brush jump rather than over it.

Luckily for me, he didn't know the layout of the outside course, so when he came to the sharp left turn just after the brush jump, he didn't know where to go next. He stopped, trembling and shaking, while he looked for a new flight path.

Before he could decide on one, I thought *"This is where I leave."* Putting the training for emergency dismounts to good use, I flew off him while I was still in one piece. We both just stood there a few moments, 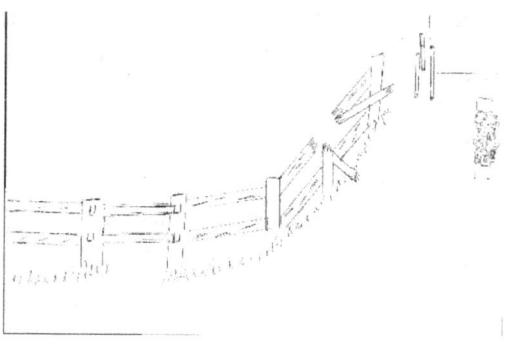 more than slightly shaken. Socks was still undecided whether he was going to continue to flee, but I managed to hold on to him until we both could start breathing normally again

Cilla was at my side almost as soon as I landed on my feet "Katlyn, are you alright? Is he OK? Are you cut from the broken fence, either of you?" The questions came faster than I could possibly answer them. As I looked at her, I saw that she was nearly as badly shaken as I was. "I saw him take off like a shot, headed straight for the gate, bars and all. He was going to jump that gate!", she exclaimed. "I was so scared you were going to go flying and be hurt!"

"I know, so was I. I was trying to turn him but he was going too fast to make the corner. Thank goodness that post broke" I replied. Grateful for her presence and support, we walked with a still excited but manageable Socks up to the barn.

Of course, there was a group of people who I had to assure that I was not hurt, just a bit shaken. Among them was Mrs. Smith, who boarded her big gray hunter 'Frosty Morn' at the barn. As Cilla and I were cooling Blaze off and getting his tack put away, I suddenly had a terrible thought. What if Mrs. Smith mentioned the incident to my father when she was at the club? The Smiths were members there as were several of the boarders. My father was forever talking to those members who had horses at the barn about how much I loved riding. And if my father knew it, you could be sure my mother would know about it too.

"Cilla, where's Mrs. Smith?" I asked.

"I don't know. Why?"

"I have to warn her not to say anything to my father. If he knows about this and tells my mother, who knows what her reaction will be. But it probably won't be good!" The very thought that she might decide that riding was too dangerous an activity for me to participate in, was terrifying and to be avoided at all costs!

Unfortunately, Mrs. Smith had already left for home.

"Cilla, this could be bad if Mrs. Smith says anything to Dad."

"Well, maybe she won't say anything. She might not think it a big deal. After all, you weren't hurt. And she thinks nothing of putting her four-year-old in the saddle on *Frosty*. She lets Sandy walk him around, big as he is, even though Mrs. Smith knows she can't stop him if he's jumping the hunt course."

I was still worried about my mother hearing about the incident as Cilla and I walked down to the ring to inspect the damaged fence.

Cilla quavered, "Oh my gosh."

What? What is it?" I queried.

I looked where she was looking to see what made her sound so scared. I gulped and was nearly sick to my stomach. We could clearly see the hoof prints where Socks had landed after breaking through the fence. They were just between some loose pipes lying on the ground beside the nursery for grass for the course greens. Had Socks landed a couple of inches in either direction from where he did, he would have landed on the loose pipes.

The area of the nursery was right next to the arena, between the ring and the edge of the hunt course field. It's presence mandated that the outside hunt course take a ninety-degree turn after the first jump to go around the nursery area. When I thought about the fall we would most certainly have taken had Socks landed on those loose pipes, I was scared all over again. Even Cilla turned a bit pale at the thought.

"I don't think we need to say anything about the pipes," I said. "I think the less said about that narrow escape, the better."

Things settled down, we ate our brown-bag lunches and were ready to take our ride. Although we had intended to go on a trail ride, after all the excitement, we settled on just fooling around in the ring and taking a walk along the hunt course I had so nearly ended up jumping! We would have our lesson tomorrow and wait until next weekend to go on a trail ride.

At the end of the day, I walked up the ninth fairway to the pro shop, waited while my father closed up the pro shop and then we went home. I still had butterflies when I thought about the day, but kept my thoughts and feelings to myself. This was definitely something that would not be discussed with my parents. Hopefully, no one else would discuss it with them either. Thankfully, that Saturday night was one of the few evenings when my mother and father were going out. No long discussions about how my day had gone were required.

Chapter 3

Sunday dawned bright and clear. Another perfect spring day. The thought crept in that tomorrow was a school day, but I shoved it aside for now. There was still a day at the barn to be had. Although our lesson with Warren was usually in the late afternoon, this Sunday it was going to be in the morning, as soon as Warren had the day's schedule organized and was free.

Cilla arrived at the barn by eight-thirty. She got out "Peso", the more advanced school horse that she had been riding in lessons and I brought out "Franc", also one of the more advanced school horses. We put them on the cross-ties to get them groomed and tacked up. If you were a boarder and called to say that you would be at the barn at say, two o'clock to ride, when you arrived, your horse would be all brushed and clean, tacked up and ready for you to mount and be on your way. For us kids, the discounted price we paid for lessons also meant that we groomed and tacked up our own horses before a lesson. I curried and brushed "Franc" and talked to him about the upcoming lesson.

Everything was pretty much OK walking down to the ring and letting the horses loosen up their muscles at the walk. Then "Franc" started to get a bit antsy. And I was starting to get tense. Cilla came alongside. "Quit holding him so tightly! He can't move and you're as stiff as a board! Relax." I looked down and saw how short a rein I had him on. No wonder he was objecting to it. We were only walking for heaven sakes!

Even though we were in the ring, Cilla who was just in front of me, observed the etiquette of the trail and called out "trotting." Ordinarily, that would not have been a problem at all. But, as she started to trot and Franc started to follow suit, I panicked. "Cilla, NO!" I yelled.

"What do you mean, "*No*," she asked as she circled back to me. " What's the problem?" I was tongue-tied. I didn't know what was the problem. I just was suddenly terrified to trot. "I don't know," I finally managed to mutter. "I don't think I can stop him if we trot." Why couldn't I stop him? I thought. It had never been a problem before, but now, suddenly it was a major issue!

"You're kidding, right?" asked Cilla, totally amazed at my answer. "No, I don't think so. My stomach is in knots and I'm scared!", I replied almost in tears.

"But you don't get scared on a horse. I've never known you to be afraid when riding. What's different today? "she asked, mystified but concerned.

"I don't know. I just know how I feel and it feels really scary. I've never been scared on a horse before but I am now. It's not too bad if we only walk. But even then, Franc is getting upset with me. What do I do?"

"I don't know." She thought about it for a minute or so. " I guess the best thing to do would be to talk to Warren about what's happening. He seems to be able to fix problems."

I certainly didn't want to admit to Warren how scared I was, but I couldn't see any way to avoid it. He had taught me from the very beginning. Now several years after first learning to ride, I could still hear him say "I see daylight" as he rode behind me on the trail when my knees came off the saddle. I thought he was wonderful and really wanted to have him proud of me. I certainly couldn't lie to him. But I couldn't just take my usual lesson as if everything was the same when it wasn't How could I?

Cilla and I talked some more about how I felt while we continued to walk the horses, waiting for Warren to come down to the ring. We finally decided that I wouldn't lie to him, just, sort of, not tell the entire story. Cilla would take her lesson and I would stay in the ring but not participate in the lesson because I still a bit "shook up" and sore from yesterday's wild ride. I'm sure Warren knew me well enough to suspect something was going on but was too wise an instructor to make an issue of the situation.

Chapter 4

The week after my *express ride* was a busy one at school. There were a bunch of weekly exams in various subjects so I didn't have much time for soul-searching. Off and on I thought about what I was going to do about how I felt. I considered quitting riding. Somehow that didn't seem to be the thing to do, I couldn't envision my life without horses. But I couldn't go to the barn, not ride, and just be a stable-hand. My mother would be horrified and never allow it. I also knew it wouldn't be enough for me. The more I thought about it, the more I realized I wanted to be a rider and trainer. To be those things, I had to be **on** a horse. That seemed to leave only one-option— figure out how to get over my fear.

I eventually came to the only conclusion possible— there was only one person who could help me get through this —Warren. Much as I might hate to admit my fear to him, I knew he would have a solution. Now to screw up the courage to admit to him how scared I was! I felt he would be so disappointed in me!

I was also anxious about whether my mother would hear about the incident. I knew I was safe until at least Thursday, the ladies golf day. It was unlikely that my father would run into Mrs. Smith before then. Maybe I'd be lucky and Dad wouldn't think anything of it even if Mrs.

Smith mentioned it. But if Dad said anything about it to Mom, that would likely be another story. I thought I would probably be safe until Friday before my mother would have anything to say to me about the crash.

I braced myself for a confrontation as I came in the house after babysitting the boys. Trying to appear casual and normal, I joined Mon in the kitchen to help get dinner ready.

"Boy, the boys were awful today." I volunteered. "I don't know how they manage to think up the things they can get into trouble over. While I was changing Mark, Paul and Peter managed to destroy a laundry basket, using it as a sleigh, before I could stop them. Good thins Mrs. M knows her boys so she wasn't mad at me."

"She isn't going to get angry with you for their mischief. She knows you are probably the only person who can control them at all." Mon said. She continued, "here, peel these potatoes please, while I get the salad started."

I would have stood on my head at that point if she had asked. Clearly, she hadn't heard anything! I was safe, at least for now.

I walked down the ninth fairway Saturday morning, tossing around a variety of thoughts about what I was going to do today. I couldn't think of anything concrete as a solution. Hopefully, Cilla would have some ideas to offer.

When Cilla arrived, we went to the rec room to talk and try to figure out what to do.

"I have an idea we could try," Cilla said. "I don't know if it will work or help but we could find out"

"I'm willing to try anything," I said.

"What horse do you trust the most of all the horses?" she asked.

"That's easy" I replied. "Pal, of course." Pal was a palomino older school horse that was used to start the itty-bits in their first times on a horse. He had 'taken care of' many, many new riders and knew that was his job.

"What if we ask Warren if you can take Pal on a trail ride for some R&R for him? But, you don't have to ride him by yourself. I will have him on a lead line, i.e. pony him, so you can see how you feel about it.

Maybe by now, it will be OK and no longer a problem, but if it is, you should feel safe on Pal with him on a lead line."

"I think that will work," I said. "At least it's a place to start. Let's go ask Warren."

Pal had no lessons scheduled until late that afternoon. Warren thought it a great idea to let him have some trail time after all the ring work. Neither one of us mentioned anything about me being on a lead line.

As we got ready to mount up Cilla said quietly "I'm not going to do anything with the lead line until be leave the barn. We will be just walking out the driveway to the trail behind the barns before we are on the actual trail. Are you OK with that?"

"Sure, that'll be fine. Pal isn't going to do anything stupid, probably not even on the trail itself, but the lead line will still be a good idea once we are in the woods." As expected Pal calmly walked along behind Cilla's horse leaving the barn. He walked with a bit more spring to his steps as he realized we were headed for the trail, not the ring, but still was the perfect gentleman.

Once on the trail, we stopped long enough for me to unhook Pal's lead from around his neck and hand the end to Cilla. I felt secure, knowing that Cilla was blocking the trail ahead of me and had firm control of Pal.

"Try a couple of walk/ halts" Cilla suggested once we were away from the barn. "See how it feels."

"OK. One, two, three, halt." I said.

Laughing, even though the lead line had pulled her half off the saddle Cilla said" I thought you said you were feeling OK? That halt was strong enough to stop an elephant. Pal practically sat down!"

"Uh, I guess I was a bit strong," I said, trying not to laugh at the position Cilla had been tugged into when the lead line had tightened so abruptly. "Guess I'm a bit more uptight than I thought I was. I'll try to be softer next time."

We continued to practice some more halts until we reached the orchard where we had decided to have lunch. It was a lovely spot, open and sunny. The trail went across the side of a gently sloping hill, well away from the traffic on the road you could see lower down. Just above the trail was a large apple orchard in full bloom. The scent of the blossoms filled the air. If we were careful not to let the horses snatch at the tree branches, when the apples were ripe, the owner didn't mind if we hand-picked a few for the horses. We took the bridles off the horses so they could graze in their halters. With a lead line attached, we could keep them from wandering too far.

As we were repacking our lunch papers and bottles, we noticed a rider trotting toward us. As he came closer, he called out "Are you, ladies, alright? I saw you standing by the horses and couldn't help but wonder if someone was in trouble."

"We're fine," Cilla answered. "We were just getting ready to leave after our picnic."

Looking at me, even though Cilla had answered him, the rider said "Oh, by the way, I don't think we've met. I'm George Peterson—but everyone calls me Pete." In her usual breezy manner, Cilla said, "Hi Pete, I'm Pricilla but everyone calls me Cilla." I knew she was expecting me to speak up and introduce myself, but I had become suddenly tongue-tied and unable to say anything. Before the pause could get too awkward, Cilla came to my rescue and said,"And this is Katlyn."

"Are you from the Country Club stables?" Pete asked, looking directly at me.

I finally found my voice and answered him. "Yes, we are. It was such a lovely day we decided to come out here for a picnic. It's such a pretty spot. We were just getting ready to go back to the barn when you came along." I wasn't normally shy so I didn't understand what had made me so hesitant to speak to him when he first arrived.

"I'm going in that direction too, for at least part of the way, mind if I ride along with you?"

I had a moment of panic. I didn't want to mention anything about being on a lead line, but I wasn't sure about riding all the way back to the barn without being on one. As if reading my mind, Cilla calmly mounted and headed out first, leaving me and Pete to follow. The trail was wide enough for a while to let Pete and I ride side by side. With Cilla clearly blocking the trail ahead I managed to act as if all was well. *We're just walking,* I kept telling myself and *just walking while we chatted with each other.* When the trail narrowed, Pete dropped behind me so I was nicely packaged between him and Cilla, which at least gave me the illusion of being safe. We were almost at the barn when Pete turned off to go to his barn. After he left, I realized that I had been so wrapped up in getting to know him, I had almost forgotten about the fact that I wasn't on a lead line!

"I think he likes you," Cilla said after Pete left.

"What do you mean," I asked, startled.

"Well, he certainly wasn't particularly interested in me. Most of his questions and answers were all directed to you. You were the one he wanted to know about, not me. Not that I mind. I mean, he seems like a nice guy but nothing special in my book."

"Well yeah, he was nice. I hope we see him again." And I left it at that. A part of me hoped that Cilla was right, that he was interested in me but even if that were true, I hadn't the slightest idea what, if anything, to do about it. The thought did occur that if I were able to ride on the trails without being afraid, I would have the chance to run into him again.

That evening, when asked about my day at dinner, I told my mom about the picnic, what fun it was to ride out with Cilla, and how pretty the orchard was. I saw no need to say anything about being on a lead line for part of the ride or that I had met a boy who seemed to like me and who I found equally likable.

Chapter 5

Friday afternoon, on my way to my room after babysitting, Mom said: "Katlyn, stay here a minute, I need to talk to you." I returned to the living room slowly— I had a feeling and not a good one, what this was going to be about.

"I spoke with Mrs. Smith yesterday. She mentioned your wild ride a week ago. Were you ever going to say anything about it?"

"What was there to say about it? It happened and it's over. No big deal."

"That's not quite what I understood from Mrs. Smith. She was very complimentary about how well you rode even though you crashed through the fence. As far as I'm concerned, good riding is all fine and well but crashing through the ring fence is something to be concerned about. You could have been badly injured."

Trying not to sound argumentative but needing to make my point, I said "Well, maybe, but I wasn't hurt at all. And Socks only had a slight nick on his shoulder where he hit the post."

My mother continued as if I hadn't said anything, "I'm certainly glad that you weren't hurt, but it just shows how dangerous riding can be, particularly if you don't own your own horse. I know that you enjoy your riding but I worry about your safety. I can't have you putting yourself in dangerous situations where you might be injured. I think that until such time as you are able to own a horse of your own, riding has to stop."

I was stunned. For a moment, I couldn't say anything. I was expecting Mom to have something to say about the incident but nothing like this! When I found my voice, I could only gasp "Mom, that's not fair! I wasn't hurt. Riding isn't that dangerous! You let Jamie still play hockey even after he had stitches when he was hit with a puck! And you let Billy play football even after the whole side of his face was cut and he almost lost an eye! You have to let me keep riding" I pleaded with tears making streaks down my face.

"The situation with your brothers is different. They are boys. No, Katlyn, riding on other peoples' horses is just too dangerous. It has to stop."

I climbed the stairs to my room dazed and in a turmoil by her decision. I would have liked to slam my door hard enough to shake the house but I knew that would only make matters worse. I was trying to control my hiccups from crying when my phone rang. It was Cilla.

"Katlyn, I won't be able to meet you at the barn until after lunch tomorrow. My brother has a game and Mom has to take him there before she can drop me at the barn."

"That's OK. I won't be at the barn tomorrow anyway." I mumbled.

"What do you mean? What's going on? You sound terrible" she asked all at once, concern clear in her voice.

"Mom heard about going through the fence. She has decided riding is too dangerous until I own my own horse so I can't ride anymore."

"Oh my gosh! She really said that? What are you going to do?"

"What can I do?" I asked helplessly. "You know my mother. Once she makes up her mind about what is best for me, that's it. You might as well try to stop the tide from coming in! Any suggestions?"

"No, not just offhand," Cilla said thoughtfully. But there must be something that can be done!"

Half-jokingly I added, "well since I won't be riding I guess I don't have to worry about not being able to stop a horse, do I?" And had to take a couple of deep breaths to stop the tears starting to leak from my eyes again.

"Katlyn, I have to go now to help with dinner, but tomorrow I will talk to Warren and see if he has any suggestions. I'll call you when I get home."

I was still hurt and angry and rebellious the next day. *How could my own mother be so mean? Couldn't she understand what riding meant to me? I was no longer a sickly little kid that had to be treated carefully. I was as healthy as my brothers. They could get hurt and not be banned from sports why not me? And I hadn't even been hurt!* My mind raged round and round with the unfairness of it all but of course, it didn't change a thing.

Saturday morning arrived but I was in no mood to be sociable. I wasn't sure I could even be polite to my mother. The simplest way to avoid any further confrontations was to stay out of my mother's way and stay in my room. To avoid being accused of "sulking", which would only make matters even worse, I tore my room apart in a flurry of cleaning and rearranging. Since it really needed a cleaning, Mon wasn't about to argue the point. While vacuuming and dusting and sorting, I waited impatiently for Cilla to call, hoping and praying that she and/or Warren would come up with a solution.

Finally, the phone rang. Without giving Cilla a chance to speak, I asked" Did Warren have any ideas? Or you? Please tell me you two found a solution!".

Cilla laughed. "Give me a chance! Yes! I talked to Warren about it. He understood how you feel, but couldn't come right out and suggest that you defy your mother, even if there was a way you could. But he did suggest that if being injured was your mother's concern, maybe if you only rode in the ring in a lesson or under some other supervision, your mother might think it safer and let you ride that way. Might that work?"

"I don't know. Maybe if I could get my father to say something. I haven't said anything to him about this whole mess yet, though I'm sure my mother has told him what she said. But, I'm the youngest and the only girl, so sometimes he lets me have my way. My brothers would say he always lets me have my way, but that's not really so. But at least he's not afraid to let us play sports so just maybe he would talk to my mother and get her to change her mind, at least enough to let me ride in the ring.

"This weekend is a loss. I won't get a chance to really talk to my father until Monday which is his day off. I don't think he has a tournament this week, so he should be home. I'll speak to him then. If luck is with me, maybe I'll see you next weekend. But I'll call you and let you know how it goes."

The remainder of the weekend dragged on. It helped some that Sunday was rainy. I consoled myself that I wouldn't have been able to ride anyway.

Monday, after babysitting, I wandered out to the backyard where my father was hitting balls into the canvas he had hung from the side of the garage.

"Can I talk to you a minute Dad?"

"Sure, what about? Though I think I know," he replied.

"Your right, it's about not riding. I know Mom loves me and is only concerned for my safety, but riding is so important to me. I can't just not be able to do it! There must be a way! What if I agreed to only ride in the ring and under supervision. Warren would be there or one of the other instructors. I wouldn't be out on the trails where anything wild could happen. And I usually ride with Cilla anyway, so someone would be with me. Surely that would be safe enough? Please, couldn't you persuade Mom to change her mind, at least a little?

After supper, before I went upstairs to finish my homework, Mom said "Katlyn your father spoke to me about your riding. We talked about ways that you might be able to keep riding that would be safe. He suggested that you ride only in the ring. But weren't you riding in the ring when you ran through the fence? That would seem to indicate that ring riding isn't necessarily all that safe."

"Yes, but Mom, I wasn't riding in a lesson and I was riding a new horse. If you let me ride again, I would only ride if Warren or one of the instructors was supervising. And I would only ride one of the horses that I usually ride. And I don't usually ride alone anyway, Cilla usually rides with me. It would be safe, really. Please?"

"Have I your word that you will have an instructor there when you ride?"

'Yes, I promise."

"And you won't ride horses you know nothing about, just the school horses or horses you are used to riding and know are safe?"

"Absolutely, I promise."

"Well, we'll try it for a while and see if it will work out. But another incident like last week and that will be it."

I gave my mother a quick hug and thank you and raced to my room to call Cilla.

"Cilla, it worked! I can ride" I almost shouted, barely giving her time to even say hello. "Dad got Mom to change her mind, at least mostly. I can only ride in the ring with supervision, but that's OK since that's all I think I can do anyway. I didn't mention anything about being scared to either Mom or Dad since there was nothing they could do about it. But at least I can work with Warren to solve that problem." I hesitated a moment, then added, "Though now that I have permission to ride, I guess I must do something about being scared, won't I?"

Chapter 6

The following Saturday as I walked down the ninth fairway, I had such jumbled thoughts and feeling, I was scarcely aware of whether it was a nice day or raining. One the one hand, I was delighted to be on my way to the barn. That had been such a terrible couple of days — thinking that I wasn't going to be able to ride.

On the other hand, what I was going to say to Warren? I tried to rehearse what I would say. Only each time I figured out what to say, it didn't sound right. Then I'd think of another way to start the conversation, but that wouldn't be right either. By the time I had walked the length of the fairway, all 396 yards of it, and arrived at the barn, I had thought of and rejected umpteen different conversations and still hadn't figured out exactly how I was going to tell Warren I was scared.

I was in luck. As soon as I got to the barn, I saw the vet was there to stitch up the leg of one of the horses had been kicked during nightly turn-out. I thought, *Warren is clearly busy! This is no time to distract him with my problems.* I asked his brother Mike "what needs doing?" and happily postponed the conversation in which I still had no idea of what to say or how to say it, as I set to work helping Mike.

Warren's twin brother's real name was Robert. I had asked Warren one day why he called his brother Bob when everyone else called him Mike. "I call him Bob because that's his name", he said. "Then why does everyone call him Mike", I asked.

"When we were little, even though his name was Robert, we were twins, so everyone started saying *Mike and Ike, they look alike* after the cartoon characters who were twins. I was Ike and Bob became Mike. I don't know why but Ike never stuck with me but Mike did to Bob, except to the family." There was just enough difference between them that it soon became easy to tell them apart.

Eventually, the morning settled down, the vet left, the trail ride went out and Warren went into the house for some coffee. I knew it was time to speak with him, though I still wasn't sure what I was going to say. I was glad he went into the house. The only person there was Hazel, his wife, and she was busy with their young baby's morning bath and feeding. I knocked and followed Warren into the house. Screwing up my courage, almost whispering, I asked, "Uh, Warren, could I talk to you about something?"

"Sure Katlyn, come on in. what can I do for you?"

I sat at the kitchen table. "Ah, I don't really know how to say this—but, remember last week when I sort-of rode Socks?

"Yes, of course, I do. You did very well, given his foolishness."

"Well, ever since then — "I'm afraid I can't stop a horse —that I'll get run away with again."

"I don't know what to do," I said, tears threatening to break through. "I can't stop riding, I just can't! But I'm so scared I won't be able to stop a horse."

"Katlyn, it's OK. Things like this happen to everyone in horses at some time or another. You're not the only one to suddenly become afraid. Horses are big animals and not always very sensible. You're just being rational to recognize their strength and have a healthy fear of what they can or might do."

I was so relieved at the normal tone of Warren's word that I hardly even took in exactly what he was saying. It was enough that he didn't even sound disappointed in me. I had been so sure that telling him would be like the end of the world, and instead, it was just another day in the world of horses!

"But what can I do about it? I don't want to stop riding, I can't-do that! But I get so scared to do anything but walk and that's not riding!. Can you fix it?"

"Katlyn, relax. It's not so big a problem that it can't be solved. You just have to take it a step at a time." reassured Warren. "Do you remember the first time you got on a horse? That was pretty scary at that time, wasn't it? To be so high off the ground on an animal that was moving underneath you? You didn't know how to stop the horse then, did you?"

"No-o-o," I drawled out but as I said it, I remembered that while it had only taken a few minutes before I thought it was great to be on a horse, those first few minutes and steps had been scary.

"So, that's what you do—go back to the beginning. Who do you most trust of all the horses in the barn-who do you think is the safest?" Warren asked.

"Pal, of course."

"Then go back to riding Pal. Get on him and pretend that you haven't been riding for the past four years. Ride him as if you had never ridden before and were just learning how to do it. Ride in the ring for a while. As you get more comfortable, I'm sure Pricilla will help you. Have her put you on a lunge line for a while until you learn to trust your seat again. In your head you know that you don't really stop a horse with the reins, you just have to believe in it again. It will take some time, but I know you can do it".

I felt so relieved, the weight of the world was off my shoulders. I didn't know *and I didn't care* whether it was because I had finally told Warren my fears or if it was because he had been so sympathetic or because there was a plan so I wouldn't have to give up riding (if it worked!). It didn't matter! There was a plan, a potential solution to my problem. And it fits within the conditions my mother had insisted on.

"Ah, Warren, there's one other thing. My mother heard about the ride through the fence. Initially, she said I couldn't ride anymore-not at all. But I managed to talk my father into coming to my rescue and he convinced her to let me ride but now there are some new rules. I can only ride in the ring, on school horses or ones I know, and it has to be under the supervision of you or another instructor. I can live with these rules, at least for now or until I find out if I can get over being scared to even ride at all."

"I don't think those new rules will be a problem, Katlyn, for now. Let's solve first things first, like basic skills and then we can worry about the rest."

I was almost skipping as I left the house, a grin from ear to ear on my face. It really was a beautiful day! I immediately went looking for Cilla. I found her in the tack room, cleaning Peso's tack.

"Cilla. I talked to Warren and told him how I felt. He wasn't surprised at all. And he doesn't think that I'm a wimp or crazy to be scared!"

"Naturally, I knew he wouldn't. That just wouldn't be Warren. I bet he had a plan in mind too, to help you get over being afraid." she said.

"Know-it-all" I snapped back, but much too happy to be anything but kidding.

Chapter 7

Later that afternoon, I tacked up Pal for the start of my "learn to ride anew" program. Warren enlisted Cilla as his assistant, to show her what to do to help me get started riding again.

As we walked to the ring, Warren explained; "First off, just some walking to loosen Pal's muscles. Once he is warmed up, then we start some walk/halt transitions."

"Katlyn is on the lunge, right? Cilla asked. "Does she have the reins?"

"No. No reins. She needs her hands free to do some exercises while she is walking and while making the transitions between gaits."

Once in the ring, Warren made Pal walk around him in a big circle. I surprised myself that I didn't feel tenser. But then again, I was on Pal and Warren had complete control of him. What was there to fear?

Warren talked about the aids for making the downward transition to a halt as Pal warmed up and as I loosened up and tried to stay relaxed.

"Ok, Katlyn now it's your turn to do something. Come to a halt while you keep your arms out to the sides—at shoulder height."

"How can I do that with my arms up high?" I asked. "Nothing will happen."

"Yes, it will, if you talk to Pal with your body, not your hands. Use your body."

I tried. I thought I was doing what Warren had said to do, but nothing happened. Pal just kept on walking the circle.

"Warren, it didn't work," I said, putting my arms down. "Now what?"

"Now you try it again, really concentrating on stopping his back, not with your hands-they need to be up high again, but just with your seat and back. Think deep, deep into the saddle. Pull in your core-take a deep breath push your heels down."

"It worked. Pal stopped!" I cried. I was so surprised and excited that he had stopped, for the moment I forgot how afraid I was that I couldn't stop a horse.

"Amazing how it works, isn't it?" Warren said.

At that point, Hazel called down to the ring. "Warren, the vet is here to see Mr. DeLong's horse."

"Cilla, take over the lunge line. Just keep Katlyn walking and making downward transitions. Don't have Pal do anything but walk but have Katlyn do all the different lunge exercises in between and during transitions. I'll be back as soon as the vet finishes." Warren said, heading for the barn.

Cilla rapid fired so many instructions at me I didn't have time to think about anything except trying to accomplish her orders. I'd barely get started on making my arms do windmills when she would ask for a transition down and then immediately back up to the walk.

"Cilla, that was four in a row that worked," I said. I'm even feeling loose and relaxed in the saddle!."

"Great. Keep that thought. she said. "It's a good place to quit and Pal's had enough of circles for one day. Let's go in."

It was a good place to quit, I thought. I felt that some hope that Warren's plan might work out and I would stop seeing that fence coming at me and hearing that crack every time I rode.

Sunday, we practiced more of the same. I did get better at the transition and was pleased with myself. There still seemed to be such a long way to go, however.

Cilla had been really patient with me, even though it was boring for her to just have me on the lunge in the ring. After she had worked with me for twenty minutes or so I said,

"Cilla" how about getting Peso tacked up, putting a lead on Pal and we take a walk in the woods. If we go to the fields, I'll get off Pal while you canter Peso for a bit. That way I don't have to be concerned that Pal will join you, but you can get a canter in."

"Sounds great. Let's go." And within a few minutes, we were on our way.

As I walked up the fairway to join my father at the end of the day, I thought about how well the two lessons had gone. If I had a fairy godmother, I thought, I would wish that tomorrow wasn't a school day and I could ride again, before I forgot what I learned yesterday and today. Unfortunately, I didn't so I couldn't, and to school I must go, waiting the eternity of six days before I could ride again. And that's if it didn't rain!

Chapter 8

As the school year neared its end, the week at school was busy. I was impatient for it to end. *Will this week never end? I need to get to the barn and see if halting still works.* Finally, it was over and I was nearly flying down the ninth fairway.

My lesson with Warren was at ten o'clock or as soon thereafter as he was free after seeing the trail ride off. Pal was ready to go as soon as Warren was free.

Warren had me walk without being on a lead line down to the ring. He walked beside me, however, as he outlined what we were going to do today. I was going to trot on the lunge.

"I don't think I can do that, Warren. Walking is getting to be pretty OK now, but anything faster and all I can see is that fence coming at me."

"It will be fine, Katlyn, you'll see. One step at a time." He put the lunge line on Pal at the far end of the ring and sent him into the circle.

"First, you do some walk/halts, to make sure those aids are still working."

Katlyn was pleased to discover that she was still able to accomplish these and stay relaxed.

"OK, those were good, "said Warren. "Now, I want you to hold on to the bucking strap while I start Pal in a few steps of trot and then I will bring him back to the walk. You don't have to do anything except believe that Pal will come to the walk when I ask him to."

I was holding on for dear life as Warren began a series of a few steps of trot then back to the walk. But I did start to realize that Pal was doing exactly what Warren asked him to do, as soon as Warren asked it. I began to sit straighter and let muscle memory help my body to relax and post the trot for the few steps Pal took.

"Good, Katlyn, you're doing fine. Next, I want you to sit up straight, try to let your body be soft and with Pal and close your eyes. What is your favorite trail?"

"Uh, the one crossing the hill below the orchard, above Elm Street."

"OK. Close your eyes, think of how that trail looks as you trot along it. Don't think of anything else. Just how it feels, trotting along that trail with the orchard slightly above, you can smell the blossoms, the breeze blows softly across your face, the sun is warm on your arms. While your eyes are closed, keep thinking about that trail while I ask Pal for a few steps of trot. I'll bring him to a walk after a few trot steps. Then ask him for a few more trot steps. I'll keep repeating the cycle until you feel comfortable with it."

"I'll try," I said, but not believing that I could do it. The first attempts were terrible. I hunched over, lost my balance and couldn't concentrate on the picture of the trail. The big screen of my mind insisted on a channel showing the ring fence breaking!

Finally, my body couldn't sustain its tightness any longer and muscle memory began to take over. I started to sit straighter and post more naturally. Suddenly my cheeks were flushed. The big screen of my mind had changed channels! As I thought of the trail, I wasn't seeing just the trail. The channel was showing a picture of Pete riding toward Cilla and me. And then the close-up as we stood talking! I hoped Warren hadn't noticed my pink cheeks.

"That's it, Katlyn, well done. Keep it up." He had noticed only that I was **riding** the trot! I was sitting up straight, my posting was rhymical, and I had loosened my death grip on the bucking strap.

I opened my eyes. This was not the time or place for that channel to play. But then, even without my eyes closed, I discovered I was able to keep riding the transitions as Warren called them out.

"One more giant step before we quit for today. You have been riding the transitions but I'm the one initiating them. Now, I want you to try to initiate them. Just concentrate on your seat bones, sitting deep, and holding your core muscles-just the same as you did at the walk. The only job of your hands is to let Pal know there is a wall in front of him that he must slow down for. You can tell him this by just closing your hands, not pulling backward. So let's try it. I'll still have you on the lunge so don't worry if it doesn't seem to work at first. I still have control of Pal if needed."

Thank goodness for that, I thought, not at all certain that I would be able to accomplish a downward transition. I was right. The first couple of times, my hands of their own volition, it seemed, pulled back to get the walk. My body leaned forward and my butt came out of the saddle. Pal stopped but gave his head a shake as if to say, 'I'll walk but that's not the way to ask for it!'

"Let's try this, Katlyn. Get your position back so you feel grounded and relaxed. Now I'll take control and ask Pal for a trot and then a down transition. As soon as he comes to the walk, you ask for the upward transition to the trot and after a few strides, you ask for the next down transition to the walk. Then, I'll ask for the trot and next downward and then it's your turn again to do the asking. Ready?"

That routine sounded a lot more doable. Warren started Pal. Knowing he was making the downward, I managed not to tense. Then it was my turn. I started to lose my position after a stride or two. Before I lost it completely, I took a deep breath and closed my hands. It worked! Pal came to a walk. We did it a few more times just to make sure I had it and then quit.

"That was well done, Katlyn," said Warren. Before I could say anything in response, I heard,

Yeah, you were terrific Katlyn." I looked toward the barn and Cilla was there. She had just come back from a trail ride with Robin and Nancy, two of our other riding buddies and had watched the end of my lesson.

"Feeling brave enough to walk around the course on your own to let Pal stretch out and relax?" she asked.

After such a good lesson, I felt I could walk on the moon. "Sure," I said, "let's go."

"Guess who we ran into on the trail today?" she asked. She had my immediate attention—I suspected and hoped I knew the answer. Before I could say anything, she added "Pete."

Aware of the sudden fluttering inside me, but trying to keep a casual tome I asked: "Oh, how is he?"

"He seemed fine. He asked about you. Where were you? How come you weren't with us."

"You didn't tell him about the lunging,?" I asked in a panic. I was sure he would be disgusted with me for being such a wimp if he knew how afraid I was.

"No, of course not! I just said that your mother had learned of an incident at the barn and had grounded you to ring riding for a while."

"Oh, thank you, Cilla. You're great."

Chapter 9

By the end of the following week, Katlyn is feeling proud of herself that she is walking and trotting and making the transitions between the gaits with a modicum of confidence. She knows, however, that this is primarily because of her confidence in Warren and Pal. Within the safety net of Warren's supervision, a babysitter school horse, and the lunge line, she is able to keep the specter of the breaking fence post at bay. But Saturday's lesson-time comes with startling news from Warren.

"Katlyn, don't tack up Pal today. Get Franc ready instead"

"Why," asked Katlyn. A thousand thoughts and excuses whirled in her mind.

"What if I can't stop Franc?" she asked." He's so much more forward than Pal. It seems that Pal listens to me now. I'm not sure that Franc will. What if he doesn't?"

"Simmer down, Katlyn." Don't make a big deal out of it. The reason for using Franc is simple. Pal is just too old to canter on a lunge line. His hocks won't take the smaller circles. And it's time to think about cantering, even if it's only on the lunge."

As we started to walk down to the ring, Warren just walking beside Franc, I said:" aren't you going to put the lead line on?"

Warren looked at me. "Should I?"

"Well, this isn't Pal," I said. "What if he starts to trot to the ring?"

"And if he does, what do you think you should do about it?" he answered.

"Ah, sit deep, take a breath, close my fingers, and say a prayer that he doesn't take off?" I answered.

"Exactly right." At that point, I realized we were already in the ring, without the lead line having been attached!

Entering the ring, I turned to Warren and said, "You know, you are really sneaky."

"Well, it worked, didn't it? Here you are, in the ring, on Franc, and you got here without a lead line."

I had to laugh. He was so right! I'd been so busy questioning him, I had just ridden Franc without giving it a thought.

But now that we were in the ring came the hard part. Warren had said I was to ride Franc because I had to canter. I wasn't at all sure that I was prepared to do that. Cantering was what I had been doing when I went through the fence. What if it happened again, only this time the post was new-maybe it wouldn't break?

I gave myself a mental shake—*That won't happen. For one thing, you are on the lunge! Besides, Warren won't let it happen.*

Patiently, Warren said, "Since you are on Franc, let's see how he responds to some transitions before we start anything new."

"OK," I quavered, "I'll try."

Disaster. Even though I had been riding Franc for a year, now I didn't trust him. As he picked up a more forward trot than Pal's lazy-daisy shuffle, I tensed, my hands became stiff and I ended up hauling on his mouth to slow him down and make him walk.

"It isn't working. I can't-do it on Franc," I said, bursting into tears as fear gripped me tightly.

Warren said nothing, giving me the time to get control of myself. As I dried my tears on my shirt-sleeve, Warren said "OK, let' look at what just happened. Franc did as you asked and started to trot. As you felt him get a bit fast, you started a fight with him with your hands. Understandable, but what should you have done? "he asked.

Still sniffling a bit, I thought about an answer. I knew what the answer should be, I just hadn't considered it in my panic.

"I should have brought him in on a smaller circle and let the figure slow him down, instead of starting a fight," I admitted.

"Right. Now let's try it again. This time, talk to Franc with your body. If he doesn't listen right away, show him what you want him to do. Even being on the lunge, you can bring him in close to me and continue circling." He can't race around on a tiny circle. "

Franc was a very willing horse, anxious to please his rider. Once I gave him a chance to be the gentleman he was, things went much better. I relaxed, he didn't fight me and we managed some nice working trot/walk transitions. I started to remember why I had liked to ride Franc so much and appreciated him anew.

As well as things were going, Warren was not about to veer from his original lesson plan. Cantering was up next.

"Katlyn, I want you to trot a few circles, then ask for a canter. From sitting the canter go into a 2-point position. You can come to the trot before you change positions if you need to, but try to just make the change of position into the 2-point.maintaining the canter. Hold on to Franc's mane if you need to maintain the 2-point without balancing on the reins. In the 2-point, make sure that all of you, from knee to knee, is touching the saddle but your butt is somewhat out of it. Don't try to canter more a few canter strides. It's the change of position and transitions that we're looking for. Remember, I still have the lunge. You concentrate on achieving your positions; I'll take care of Franc."

One thing about Franc that helped settle me enough to even try the exercise was I knew how good he was about taking the aids to canter quickly and easily. No trotting faster and faster until he finally fell into a canter. If he had done that, I knew I would never have been able to canter him.

Warren made sure that there were only a couple of canter strides before he brought Franc to a trot for the first few tries. I barely had time to start to tense before there was a transition and Franc and I were safely trotting. With patience and subtleness, Warren soon had me cantering full circles in each position before I realized it.

Warren said that was enough for one day. I started to walk Franc in the ring to cool him down when I realized a horse and rider had been watching the end of the lesson. With the lesson over, he approached the ring to ride along with me. It was Pete.

What can I say to him? Obviously, he saw that I was on the lunge line. What must he think? All kinds of explanations raced through my mind. But I still didn't know what to say.

"Hi," he said as he came alongside Franc. Indicating Franc, he added, "He OK with a strange horse next to him?"

"Ah, yeah, sure—he's fine." That question I could answer.

"Was that Warren teaching the lesson? He is a really good teacher. No wonder you made such progress in the lesson."

I found my voice sufficiently to ask, "How much of the lesson did you see?"

I cringed when he said, "about half of it." No chance that he was unaware of the fact that I was on a lunge line.

"That 'incident' that Cilla said your mother grounded you for, have anything to do with being on the lunge line?" he asked, not as if he was trying to pry, just part of a conversation.

I hesitated and then decided that I might as well 'fess up and tell him what happened. So, I told him the whole story and how scared I was and still was, that I would be run-a-way with again.

"I can't say that I have ever crashed through a fence on a bolting horse," Pete said, "but I can imagine how scary it must have been. I can think of several people I know that would never have gotten on a horse again."

I let out the breath I had been almost holding, and smiled. The thoughts flashed through my mind faster than I could acknowledge them. *He wasn't disgusted with me. He didn't think I was a wimp for being on a lunge line. He still liked me!* There was someone else I could talk to about my fears without them being critical of me.

It was time to bring Franc into the barn. Before he left Pete said "I guess if you can't leave the ring, I will have to come by this way more often. Check out how the battle is coming. Maybe we could have lunch together here?"

"Sure, that would be great. There is a machine in the rec room that has cokes and chips and stuff. Cilla and I always bring a brown bag lunch. I'm hoping too, that I can soon go back out on the trails. I have to win some further negotiations with my mother before that can happen but I'm working on it. But it would be fun if you could visit here."

Cilla hadn't been able to come today so she was unaware of Pete's visit. I couldn't wait to call her to tell her all the details.

Chapter 10

Katlyn walked into the ring to start her lesson. To her surprise, Warren did not step forward to attach the lunge line. A turning point in Katelyn's lessons had arrived. Although she could now walk, trot and canter, still only on the lunge. It is time to go on her own.

"Take Franc to the rail, Katlyn and let him lengthen into a nice long walk stride." Directed Warren.

"Aren't you going to put me on the lunge? I questioned.

"Do you think it necessary for now?"

"Well, maybe not if I'm just walking" I had to admit.

"Then just walk with some halt transitions and see how it goes."

Surprising myself, I did manage several smooth transitions.

"Now, while walking, go up into your 2-point position and do a couple of transitions," Warren asked.

I figured I could do that since Franc and I were still just walking and I did.

Warren waited until we had gone past the corner with the new post before he said "Close your legs softly and ask for only four trot steps, no more, before walking again.

Taking a deep breath, I thought, *surely, I can manage four steps. How much could go wrong in four strides?* I closed my legs but I closed my eyes as well. I started to count strides. As I started to say four, my hands closed, my heels went down and it worked! Franc returned to a walk. Opening my eyes, I realized I also had pasted a big smile on my face. We had done it.

The rest of the lesson was spent practicing transitions between gaits. I was beginning to feel as if I was truly riding again, but I knew I was fooling myself. Warren was still figuratively holding my hand, even if I wasn't on the lunge. The safety of a solid fence containing the horse so he had no place to go except within the ring, provided me with a sense of security that was outside of myself. And I hadn't yet cantered off the lunge.

Cilla had come in from a trail ride and watched the tail end of my lesson. She came over while I was putting Franc away.

"I watched you at the last part of your lesson. You were doing great—no lunge."

"Oh, Cilla, it's taking so-o-o long. I'm still in the ring, I haven't cantered without the lunge and I am not at all sure that I will ever be able to canter, on or off the lunge without seeing that barred gate rushing at me and hearing that post break. I am so discouraged. I might as well accept the fact—I'm not ever going to be able to ride the way I did, so I might as well quit now."

"Katlyn, don't say that. Don't even think it. You are too good a rider to quit riding. You are making progress. I can see it. Ask Warren, he'll tell you too. I know, it must seem awfully slow, but you are improving each week." Cilla chided.

She continued, "Somehow you have to erase that picture and sound, get them completely out of your head. I wish I could tell you how to do that. I can't, but I'm sure that is what you have to do."

"I suspect you are right," I said. "I just wish I knew how to accomplish it."

Changing the subject, Cilla asked, "When does Mrs. Pierson leave for the summer?"

"Not for another couple of weeks, after we are out of school. And speaking of Moonbeam, that's another thing. How am I going to be able to ride in the Fall show? I need to be able to ride off a lunge and out of the ring to do that. Mrs. Pierson is great to have offered to let me ride her horse, Moonbeam, while they are away in Maine for the summer and to show him in the Fall show. But unless something changes quickly, including my mother's rules, how am I going to pull that off?"

"We can figure out a way," Cilla said, "Moonbeam would be perfect for you. Mrs. Pierson is a lovely lady, but she's not a brave rider, she just likes to trail-ride. Moonbeam is flashy enough to show, he's a handsome dark bay tobiano. He is kind and doesn't have a shy or spook or bolt in him. You know he is lazy enough that he is going to stop cantering the minute that you stop insisting that he keep cantering. There is virtually no risk that he won't stop, which is exactly what you need.  Would Mrs. Pierson let you start to ride him now, in lessons even though they haven't left yet?

"It might be a problem for another week or two, but then we'll be out of school and I can ride during the week. Mrs. Pierson never rides except on the weekends, so if I rode him once during the week, it wouldn't inconvenience her. And then they would be gone so I could ride him weekends too."

Katlyn added "Mom's restrictions don't have anything to do with which horse I ride. So, as long as I continue riding in the ring, under supervision, there's no reason why I can't ride Moonbeam. "That would be one step toward cantering. and getting ready for the Fall show.

Chapter 11

Kathlyn approached Warren as soon as she arrived at the barn the following Saturday.

"Warren, Cilla and I were talking about the Fall show. You know Mrs. Pierson said I could ride Moonbeam this summer while they were away and then show him at the show?"

"Yes, Katlyn, Mrs. Pierson spoke to me about it. Sounds like a good idea and a good match."

"What I was wondering was if there is a Saturday or Sunday when you know Mrs. Pierson isn't going to ride and if it's OK with her, could I take my lesson on Moonbeam?" I asked.

"Well, she is going to be here shortly, so you could ask her. It would certainly be fine with me. And if she rides today, it's unlikely she will ride tomorrow so maybe we could use Moonbeam in tomorrow's lesson He would be perfect to start cantering off the lunge."

Needless-to-say, Mrs. Pierson being the wonderful lady that she was, had no problem letting me ride Moonbeam so long as it didn't interfere with her riding schedule. Riding him for my lesson the next day would be fine. Now that I had carefully gotten everything arranged, I had to face the fact that I was committed to cantering Moonbeam off a lunge the following day.

It made for a night of fitful sleep. One moment I was pleased that I would be riding Moonbeam—I really did like to ride him—and fall asleep. Then I would wake from a dream of hurling through the fence again.

I talked to myself all the way down the ninth fairway the following morning. *Cantering on Moonbeam would be OK. He was sensible and kind. He would listen. And, of course, Warren would be there.* It was a good talk, but I wasn't sure that I had completely convinced myself.

Lesson time arrived. Moonbeam was tacked up, Warren was ready—*show-time*, I thought.

The warm-up part of the lesson went well. Moonbeam was a gentleman, responding well to my aids.

"Alright, Katlyn, from a nice working trot, with an even tempo, send him into a canter but only for five or six strides, then bring him back. As you come around the corner, leg yield him into the corner to help balance him as you ask for the canter."

Easy for you to say, hard for me to do, I thought, as I tried to execute the instructions. Moonbeam, however, had his own version of the drill. Whether it was because he knew with Mrs. Pierson he could make her ask several times before he gave in and cantered or whether it was because I was so tentative with my aids and tense, the canter wasn't happening. By the time we finally started to canter, we were heading right for 'the awful corner'.

The new post and rails were stark, raw wood. The wood preservative had to be absorbed and dry before they could be painted. The new wood in sharp contrast to their pristine white neighboring boards stood out like neon signs. Neon signs that my mind read as *Stop! Now!* Which is exactly what I did. I closed my hands and pulled back hard. Moonbeam apparently thought that such a strong halt signal meant a strong halt. He planted his front feet and stopped.

As I righted myself from around his neck— I had almost gone over his head to the ground— Warren, said, trying to keep a straight face, "That was impressive. I would say he knows a halt aid, wouldn't you?"

I didn't know whether to laugh or cry. It really was comical, I had to admit. But at the same time, I was embarrassed that I had so overreacted. That the sight of the new post and boards had caused such a reflex.

"OK, back to business, Katlyn. Ride a circle at the far end of the arena, away from the gate. Concentrate on making the transition to the canter. Moonbeam needs to know that when you apply the aids, it means now, not three or four tries later. Keep him on the circle, canter only half the circle and then down to trot."

The circle at the far end of the arena kept me from having to look at the fence repairs. I concentrated hard on getting Moonbeam to make prompt, smooth transitions in and out of the canter, as well as to stay on the circle. Cantering in the customary circle, I forgot that the lunge line wasn't attached. I was too busy trying to gain Moonbeam's cooperation to think about the fact that I was cantering on my own, without the lunge line.

While I was untacking Moonbeam after the lesson, Warren was getting a boarder's horse ready to for its owner. As we were grooming the horses, he asked, "Are you still planning on showing Moonbeam in the Labor Day show, Katlyn?"

"I hope to" I answered. "That is if I can get my act together by then and ride like I'm supposed to."

"If that's the case, then I think that you need to have another conversation with your mother. Even if you are ready, I doubt that Moonbeam can be ready if he is only ridden in the ring. You both need some trail time to prepare for a solid show performance. Remember, there will be spectators at ringside, as well as other distractions and noises typical of a show. You need to make sure that he will pay attention only to you and trust you to take care of him, no matter what else is going on. You won't be able to do that if he has only been ridden in the ring."

"I hadn't thought about that," I said. "Now that you say it, I know you're right. I know it is also necessary for me. I've gotten to feel pretty secure riding in the ring and walking the hunt course. But, deep down, I know it's because people are around me to see that nothing bad happens and the horses I'm riding feel at home in the ring and the barn fields. I guess I'll have to talk to her."

I had talked to myself all the way down the ninth in the morning. Now I was talking to myself all the way back up the ninth to go home.

Different subjects but the same upset and turmoil. *What on earth could I say that would get my mother to loosen up her rules? If she didn't, bye-bye horse show. I'd still have Moonbeam to ride all summer as if he were mine, but to what point?*

I stopped dead in the middle of the fairway. *Maybe that was the key,* I thought. *As if he were my own!* I resumed walking as I mulled over this new approach. Mom was concerned with safety and she thought that having your own horse would be safer. Could I convince her that having Moonbeam for the summer was like having my own horse and therefore, it wasn't risky to go out on the trails with him?

I had some time to think about this before I approached my mother with it. Time to talk to Cilla and see what she thought of it and what suggestions she might have. Maybe there was a ray of hope starting to shine through.

Chapter 12

Katlyn and Cilla are about to have lunch in the rec room and brainstorm an approach to Mrs. Lange when a horse and rider approach the barn. It was Pete.

Cilla called out to him, "Hey, Pete. Put your horse in an empty stall and join us. We are about to have lunch." After taking care of his horse, Pete joined them in the rec room. "Lunch is waiting for me when I get home, but I'll have a coke with you. I just stopped in to say hello and see how everything was going. Still making progress, Katlyn?"

"Progress yes, but another roadblock," I said. "I'm feeling pretty good off the lunge here at the barn and ring, but the real test will be out on the trail. I have yet to go on a trail to find out if I can ride outside a ring. But, my mother's rules include no trail riding. And to make it worse, I can't get Moonbeam ready for the Fall show unless I can take him on the trail."

"Katlyn has an idea that might work to get her mother to change the rules." offered Cilla. "Mrs. Pierson is letting Katlyn ride her horse, Moonbeam, all summer while they are away in Maine. So, for the summer it will be like Katlyn has her own horse. Mrs. Lange concern is safety; she thinks that riding a horse that isn't your own is too dangerous.

"We were just talking about whether Mrs. Lange might be persuaded that having Moonbeam for the summer would be almost like having her own horse, so it wouldn't be dangerous to take him on the trails. And if she still promised not to ride alone, there would little or no risk of being hurt. What do you think? Might it work?"

"I don't know Mrs. Lange, but if she feels that riding your own horse is less dangerous than riding school horses, it might. Katlyn, does she know Moonbeam?" asked Pete.

"No, I don't think so," said Katlyn. "I might have mentioned him but I don't think she has ever seen him. She does know Mrs. Pierson, though. She knows how gentle a person she is. I think Mom must know that any horse Mrs. Pierson owned and rode would have to be really quiet and safe."

"What if you could get your mother to watch you ride Moonbeam. Might that show her how safe he is?" offered Pete.

Katlyn laughed and said "Of Course, that's it! And she can't refuse to come watch me ride him. Even Mom wouldn't try to maintain he was dangerous to ride if she had never seen him.'" She almost jumped up to give Pete a hug but was suddenly overcome with shyness. All she could do was hope he understood how she felt.

Just then a car pulled in and honked. Cilla looked out. "Darn, Mom said she would pick me up early today, but I didn't think it would be this early! I must go. See you Saturday. Call me if you talk to your mother before then, Katlyn."

Alone with Pete for the first time, Katlyn didn't know what to say. She didn't usually have any problem talking to people but with Pete, she suddenly had no conversational skills. Luckily, Pete had no such problem.

"When does your school get out for the summer, Katlyn?"

This next week. We only have a half week and we're finished," I said.

"What are you going to do for the summer, when school is out?" he asked. "Since you have Moonbeam to ride, I guess you aren't going to go away."

"No, I have a job babysitting two boys from New Jersey. Their family comes to the beach for the summer. I'll have Wednesdays off as well as Saturday and Sunday. Mr. Sheffield comes up from New York every weekend. He wants to spend time with the boys so they don't need someone on the weekend, except sometimes on a Saturday night. What about you? Will you work full-time at the pharmacy during the summer?"

"Yeah, I'll be working full-time but not a straight nine to five day, every day. The schedule is flexible. I'll have to work some nights, but that's Ok because it means I'll have some daytimes when I can ride. If something important comes up, I can always swap times with one of the other guys. Dad doesn't really care who works what hours, just so long as the right number of people are working the hours the pharmacy is open.

"Hey, I'm going to be late for lunch. I better get going." He said. As we both stood, he put an arm casually around my shoulder, gave a quick squeeze and left the room to get his horse. I stood there, like the proverbial deer in headlights, surprised but delighted at the gesture, thoughts, and emotions in free-fall. It did occur to me while Cilla was a very good friend, sometimes it turned out to be nicer when she wasn't there.

Chapter 13

Sunday night after dinner, while she and her mother cleaned up the kitchen, Katlyn thought, would be a good time to broach the subject of new rules with her mother. She hoped her main argument that Moonbeam would be very close to having her own horse would be persuasive. As she loaded dishes into the dishwasher, she said, "Mom can I talk to you some more, about the rules for my riding?"

Startled at the request Mrs. Lange hesitated, a load of dishes in her hands. "Of course, Katlyn. What about them?"

"I need you to change them, or at least, some of them," Katlyn blurted out.

"I don't know what you mean," Mrs. Lange replied as she placed the dishes in the racks. "What do you want to be changed? And why? You are able to ride and that's what you wanted, wasn't it?"

"Well, yes, but I can't ride just in the ring forever, never going on the trail. Now that Mrs. Pierson has let me ride her horse, Moonbeam, and to show him at the Fall show, I need to get him schooled and in shape for the show. To do that, I need to be able to go out on the trail."

"Katlyn, you know how I feel about your riding horses, particularly ones you don't own."

"I know, Mom, but that's the point. Riding Moonbeam would be as if I had my own horse. Dr. and Mrs. Pierson are away for the whole summer. No one else will be riding him except me. Besides, you know Mrs. Pierson. She would never own a horse that was dangerous in any way. And I promise I wouldn't ride alone on the trail. I would always be with someone else. Please?"

"Katlyn, I don't see that riding Mrs. Pierson's horse changes anything. Riding horses is a dangerous activity. And horses and riding to the degree of involvement that you seem to want just is not suitable for a properly brought up young lady. Riding in the ring under supervision will have to be enough."

Katlyn paused, reorganizing her thoughts and arguments. *I must win this argument. Even though I can't say anything about it to Mom, I have to have the chance to find out if I'm brave enough to ride on the trail again.* Aware that tears and tantrums will not sway her mother, Katlyn tries another approach.

"Mom, I've always tried to do what you wanted me to. And, I'm sorry that I'm not the daughter that you envision—one who played with dolls, likes dressing up, can't wait to wear make-up—but I'm not, that isn't me. I can't be that sort of girl.

"Horses may not end up being my whole life, but, I know me well enough to know that they will certainly always be a very important part of it. I'm not a baby anymore. It won't be very long before I am off to college on my own.

"You are putting Moonbeam in the 'dangerous' category and you have never even seen him or me riding him! That's not fair."

"Katlyn, fair or not, that's my decision. No trail riding."

Katlyn avoids looking at her mother. Katlyn loves her mother and believes that her mother really does love her— but clearly, she doesn't know or understand her. Katlyn is beginning to question if her mother ever will.

"Then I guess there isn't anything more to say. Your rules will stand for now and for the next long three years. But, the minute I am eighteen, I am out of here. I will be out of the house, and on my own, no matter what it takes to accomplish it.

Katlyn tossed "I have homework to finish." over her shoulder as she retreated to the solace of her room.

Thank goodness, tomorrow is Monday, Katlyn thought, once in the haven of her room. *I'll be gone all day! I'm so angry at Mom. I don't think I could bear to be in the same house with her.* Her thoughts tumbled in disarray as she laid out the things needed for the beach tomorrow. *How could she be so rigid? Doesn't she know me at all?* She paused— a distressing thought— *Does Mom even love me? She says she does but then she does something like this. How can I believe her when her actions are so hurtful? She could have met me half-way. But, no, it can only to be all her way! Well, maybe for now, but not forever. I don't know how I am going to get through the next few days, never mind three years. but I will.*

Once in bed, sleep did not come easily. *There has to be a way. Something has to give. I won't ride only in the ring forever. But, of far more importance, I must discover whether I can ride a horse without the safety net of an arena fence to control him.* Finally, she slept.

Marge is stunned by Katlyn's determined stand. She wasn't prepared for Katlyn's show of independence. *"What just happened?"* she asks herself, as she finished loading the dishwasher. *"Could Katlyn really mean what she said? No, of course not. She is only a child. Tomorrow it will be something else."*

Shortly after Katlyn had gone to her room, Marge said, "Jerry, I had a very disturbing conversation with Katlyn earlier. It really upset me."

"Why, what happened?

"Katlyn asked me to let her go out on the trails with Mrs. Pierson's horse. You know she has him to ride all summer, while they are in Maine."

"Did she have a reason for wanting to expand the rules, for permission to go out on the trails? I know you don't think it is a very safe idea."

"She said that to get Moonbeam, Mrs. Pierson's horse, ready for the Fall show, she has to be able to school him in places other than the ring."

"Do you doubt her reason?"

"No-o-. I think that is her real reason. She continued, "I told her what she already knew, that I thought riding out on the trails, without supervision was too dangerous. So, no, she still couldn't, even on Mrs. Pierson's horse. I didn't say it to her, but it wouldn't be the end of the world if she didn't have him ready and so didn't ride in the Fall show."

"How did she react?" asked Jerry.

"That is what is so disturbing and has me so upset. She gave me another list of reason why it would be safe. When I still said no, she just looked at me for a few seconds, not saying anything. Then she announced she would be leaving home the minute she was eighteen. She said it would be a long three years until then. At the time, I didn't think she meant it. But the more I think about it, the surer I am that she did mean it, every word!"

"Well Marge, it's your rule and decision. I won't over-rule it. But if you believe not being able to ride in the Fall show when she finally has a horse available to her that is up to the job, wouldn't be the end of Katlyn's world, I think you are very wrong. And, from what you have told me, I think she has just told you as much."

"What do you mean?"

"I mean, is it worth losing your daughter over? If she spoke of leaving as soon as she is eighteen, I, for one, would believe her. Remember, she is my daughter too. When I said I was leaving home, I meant it. And I was only fourteen. I never changed my mind and I never regretted it. Oh, I've sometimes had second thoughts about how it would have been handy to have a high school diploma. But never my decision to leave.

"From what everyone tells me, Katlyn not only loves horses but she is also a gifted rider. She has a natural seat and hands. I don't know exactly what that means, but I gather it is something you are born with.

Becoming a professional horseperson may not be what you planned for Katlyn, Marge, or even like to think of as happening, but it may well be what Katlyn is meant to be." With that said, Jerry stood and headed for the stairs. "Come-on, time for bed," he said.

Marge toss and turned most of the night. *How could Katlyn say such a thing? Did she truly mean it? Was Jerry right? Would she lose her only daughter over a trail ride? Maybe Katlyn was more like her father than she thought. He was as easy-going about most things as a man could be but then there was golf—he could be implacable on that subject. Was Katlyn like that—easy-going until you ran into something that really and truly mattered to her and then wham, you hit a stone wall?*

Putting all the pieces together, Marge acknowledges there is only one conclusion; Katlyn means it! Marge realizes that to continue along her stated path, she may lose her daughter, not only in three years but starting now.

What could she do about it? What should she do about it? The questions whirled endlessly throughout the night. Morning's arrival offered no solution.

Chapter 14

In the morning, Katlyn slipped out of the house, intent on avoiding her mother on her way to take care of the boys. The house their parents had rented for the summer was only two blocks away, an easy walk. Fortunately, the boys were active kids. Keeping track of them and keeping them safe at the beach was a full-time job that left no time for other thoughts or problems.

That evening, after a very silent dinner on Katlyn's part, Mrs. Lange said "Katlyn your father and I spoke last night about the conversation you and I had. After my discussion with him, I realize I may have spoken too hastily about you going out on the trail. Perhaps we should talk about it further."

Katlyn looks at her mother in surprise and with dawning hope. *Is it possible her mother is backing down? Changing her mind?*

"What more do you want to know?" Katlyn asked, trying very hard not to sound confrontational, although that was how she was feeling.

"Why don't you start by telling me just what you need to do for the Fall show and how you would go about doing it?".

Amazed at the turn in direction by her mother but eager to benefit from it, Katlyn replies; "Well, the most important thing is to get

Moonbeam listening just to me. To do that, he needs to experience different noises and scenes so he learns to trust me to keep him safe. We can't accomplish that if we only ride in the ring.

"Also, I would really like you to watch me ride him. I know if you watched us, you would see there is nothing to worry about. He is so sensible and quiet, he takes everything in stride. Besides, you know Mrs. Pierson, she wouldn't ride any other kind of a horse! You could pick me up on Wednesday early enough that you could see me ride before we go home."

"I can do that," her mother agreed. It will also give me a chance to talk to Warren. I still don't want you riding alone or on other horses unless Warren says it's safe. We can talk some more about this after Wednesday."

Katlyn can't wait to phone Cilla to tell her the new turn of events. Cilla barely has answered when Katlyn babbles in one non-stop breath, "Cilla, she maybe is going to change her mind. Mom's going to talk to Warren on Wednesday," And proceeded to relate the conversation with her mother, piece by piece.

"I won't know for sure how much Mom will relent until after she watches me ride and speaks to Warren on Wednesday. But if it includes trail riding, wouldn't that be great?."

Katlyn then added, "Course I still don't know if I will have a major meltdown once I'm not on a lead line out on the trail. I guess it's like the chicken and the egg; I won't know if I can ride out on the trail unless I can get to the trail!"

Cilla interrupted Katlyn's continuous flow of works adding, "Don't forget to remind Warren that your mother knows nothing about how scared you were and what you have been doing about it, before your mother talks to him."

"Oh my gosh, I forgot all about that. Thanks for reminding me. The last thing Mom needs to know is that I might be scared to go out on the trail! I'm sure Warren won't mention it. And since Mom knows nothing about that part of it, neither will she. I'll call you as soon as I know anything more."

Tuesday seemed very long to Katlyn as if it would never end and get to Wednesday. The boys were full of mischief. The water at the beach was flat and very cold with the onshore breeze. As it always seemed to be when the water was its coldest, the sun was its hottest. However, there were a lot of castles to be built and knocked down and tide pools in the rocks to be explored. But at last, the day was over. The boys were cleaned up and returned to their mother's care. Now, just dinner and the evening to get through.

Finally, it was Wednesday.

Before Dad and I left for the club, Mom said, "I'll come to the barn about two-thirty, Katlyn. I'll watch you ride, speak with Warren and we'll be home in time to start dinner"

"That should be fine," I said.

I had Moonbeam ready to ride by the time my mother showed up. I said a silent prayer of thanks to Warren that I could now ride by myself to the ring and school Moonbeam in all three gaits, even if dependent on the security of the arena fence. The past several rides, Moonbeam had acted bored by all the ring work. Today, as if he knew he was on trial or in some kind of a test, he was perfect. Never once did he dispute anything I asked of him and he executed every request promptly. It just wasn't possible that my mother could think him dangerous as she watched me ride him.

I was hoping I would be part of the discussion Mom had with Warren. Not to be. As soon as I finished riding, she and Warren disappeared into his office. I had to untack and rinse off Moonbeam before putting him to bed. By the time I was finished, Mom came out of Warren's office. I had reminded Warren not to say anything about me being scared and I was sure he hadn't, but what else had they talked about?" Maybe Mom would tell me on the way home. Although when you came right down to it, all I really wanted was a "Yes, you can trail ride Moonbeam." Any other conversation was irrelevant.

Chapter 15

Much as I wanted to just blurt out "Well, may I trail ride?" as we started home, I knew that wasn't the thing to do. That wasn't the way you approached subjects with Mom. Difficult as it was, I said nothing about her conversation with Warren. Instead, I asked, "What did you think of Moonbeam? Isn't he great?"

"He is very pretty. I can see why you would think him suitable to go into a horse show. And he certainly seemed to do just what you wanted him to do. Warren was very complimentary about him and how well you rode him."

"Moonie is a neat horse and fun to ride." I volunteered.

"Warren also explained a bit more about the program needed to get ready for the Fall show."

I held my breath waiting to hear Mom's reaction to that part of their conversation.

"I must admit that after speaking with Warren, I feel much better about your riding Moonbeam. According to Warren, it would be hard to find a safer horse. That being the case, if you will promise me that you will not ride on the trails alone and not ride other horses, even in the ring, unless Warren says it's OK, then I guess it will be alright for you to go out on the trails."

I could have jumped for joy except, of course, strapped in a seat belt made that impossible. Nor could I throw my arms around Mom and give her a big hug, since she was driving. But I did have an ear to ear grin and could exclaim "Thank you! Thank you! Thank you!"

I babbled the rest of the way home. 'It will be great to be able to trail ride with Cilla. I really have missed riding with her. But it wasn't fair to ask her to always stay in the arena just because that was where I had to ride. I can really get to work on preparing Moonie for the show now. I'm sure he will do well in the show. It will be fun to see Alice again at the Fall show. I hoped she would be entered. Though I was almost certain she would be. After all, our show was one of the major shows on the circuit. She was fun to be with, even though we only got together at the major shows."

Mom was very relieved to arrive at the house if only to have some peace and quiet. I immediately headed for my room to call Cilla to tell her I was sprung, I could trail ride again—that is if I was brave enough to do it.

Mrs. Lange, released from the incessant chatter of the ride home, enjoyed the sudden quiet of the kitchen. Peeling the potatoes for dinner, she thought about the change that had come over Katlyn once she had been told she could trail ride. *Jerry was right. I almost lost my daughter. I never realized how important riding was to her. I had always thought that being a girl automatically made her like me—outgoing, wanting to be involved with people, doing what the rest of the crowd was doing. But that's not Katlyn. She is her father's daughter. She can easily connect with people, but she doesn't need them. She needs only her own goals and accomplishments. Perhaps now that I understand her better, I will be able to better appreciate how dedicated and skilled she is. But horses are still dangerous and I do worry about her being hurt. I just want to keep her safe!*

Katlyn sitting cross-legged on her bed, phone in hand, dialed Cilla. *Please be home. I'll burst if I can't tell you, right now!* she thought as the phone rang and rang.

Finally, Cilla answered. "And???" which was all she needed to ask.

"Warren did it! I can go out on the trail with Moonbeam, so long as I don't ride alone. But I wouldn't trail ride alone anyway, so that's no problem."

"Wow! That's terrific. Think about where we will go on Saturday. A picnic at the orchard?" asked Cilla.

"That might be a bit far out." offered Katlyn, envisioning the wide, open spaces of that trail and how far from the barn the orchard was. Ah, maybe something a little closer to home for the first time?"

"Sure, whatever you think. It will be great to be able to go into the woods at all, who cares what trail. Think about it and we'll decide Saturday. See you then."

Katlyn did think about leaving the barn area to go out on the trails off and on during Thursday and Friday. One part of her couldn't wait. The other part of her didn't know if she was brave enough to take the risk that something might go wrong. *If something goes wrong,* she thought, *would she be right back where she had been when she crashed through the fence? Even Moonbeam isn't perfect.*

By Friday night, the only solution Katlyn had was to go to Warren. The more she thought about the pros and cons involved, the more she realized a plan was necessary. Warren had devised a plan of action to get her started on the road back, surely, he could suggest a plan for this next phase of her rehabilitation.

Chapter 16

As soon as Katlyn arrived at the barn on Saturday, she sought out Warren.

"Warren, thank you, thank you so much. Mom changed her mind. I can take Moonbeam on the trail. Cilla and I can ride together again." She hesitated. "But, there's a problem. What if I can't do it? What if Moonbeam takes off? I have to find out if what I can do in the ring, I can do without a fence around us. But, I'm still scared of what might happen," she confessed. "I don't know where to start."

"Of course you do, Katlyn," Warren replied, continuing to tack up Mrs. Howe's horse. She was due to arrive momentarily. "You start at the beginning, just like you did before. You take baby steps, then toddler steps, and then bigger ones until you are there, taking grown-up strides. If Cilla rides ahead of you and you avoid the open fields, where can Moonbeam go? He's not alpha enough to push his way past Peso, so he'll just follow along, doing whatever Peso does."

"You make it sound so simple. I wish I could be sure it was that simple. When Cilla arrives, could you tell her what you just told me, so she'll know what to do when we go out?" I asked.

"Not a problem, Katlyn. Let me know when you are ready to go out."

When Cilla arrived, I said, "I've thought about where we should go today. I also talked to Warren about how excited I am about being able to go on the trail but at the same time, I'm scared.

"Warren said he would talk to both of us about how to go about these first rides on the trail so that nothing scary or bad happens," I said. "If he's not too busy, we could talk to him now and then get the horses ready."

When we caught up with him, Warren interrupted his schedule long enough to patiently explain the steps to be taken. Just as when I had started in the ring, Cilla and I would repeat the process on the trail. Slowly building from simple walk/halt transitions to ones in other gaits in an orderly progression. *Warren is such a great instructor!* I thought. *I don't think I could have gotten through this without him. I know now I can at least ride in an arena, even if I find out I'm not brave enough to go on the trails.*

Mounting up, I said, "Let's walk in the ring for a few minutes. Moonbeam has never been out with Peso before. Let them get used to each other." We walked the horses side by side. They were content to walk next to each other. I said, "how about we take the short loop first. Then, if everything is OK, we can branch off and do the main loop before we head back.

We left the ring heading out the front driveway and across the street to the short loop trail. The trail ran just inside an old stone wall which separated it from the road. It had been built around1925 but was still intact albeit, with a ragged top, the result of storm-tossed branches knocking a stone off to lie at the base, here and there. The right side of the trail was bounded by the rough of the eighth fairway. Once across the street, we stopped to check the fairway for golfers. They had the right-of-way, so if anyone was coming down the fairway, you had to wait until they waived you through.

Today, no one was on the fairway so we turned left at the wall and walked along, enjoying the warm sunshine and sweet smell of the freshly mowed fairway. Every once in a while Cilla would call out "prepare to halt,—halt" to establish that the ring drills of transitions worked just as well on the trail.

Cilla asked, "How about trying just a short trot as we approach the main loop? The horses know they have to walk when we get there, so they will be ready to stop trotting even if we didn't ask them to."

The moment she mentioned 'trot' I could feel my stomach clench. My first inclination was to object—"no way!" But, I knew she was right. It was only a short section of trail she was talking about. And, after all, Peso was in the lead, blocking the trail.

"How about just a slow jog?" I replied, trying to keep my voice from quavering.

"Sure, Peso has a killer jog. Ready?" She set off as promised, in a steady, quiet jog.

A trot where no one was asking him to put much energy into it, suited Moonbeam. He ambled off after Peso, in no hurry to go anywhere, following behind happily. I managed to let go the breath I was holding and locked my hands in Moonbeam's mane so they didn't do anything foolish like haul on his mouth! Almost before I had time to realize I was trotting and breathing normally the horses came to a walk and stopped as if to ask 'OK, which trail do we take?'

Cilla turned in the saddle, "You OK?" she asked.

About to answer, 'not really', I paused and didn't say it. I realized that wasn't the right answer. I was fine! With a grin, I said, "Yeah, I'm OK. Actually, better than OK. I was tense but not panicked! I think I would call it one of Warren's 'baby steps' but at least it was steps."

"There are a couple of short stretches of the main loop that we can jog on the way in. You can get some more practice before we call it a day. Wait 'till you tell Warren!"

Just as we came to the point where the main loop rejoined the trail back to the barn, we met another rider.

"Hey, look who is out on a trail." It was Pete. "What happened? I thought you were grounded."

Beaming, I shared the news of my reprieve. Of course, my evident pleasure had nothing to do with seeing Pete again. It was completely related to my good news. I could tell that to myself, but from Cilla's expression, she certainly wouldn't believe it if I said it to her. We rode back to the barn together, catching up with each other's lives since we had last met.

Before Pete headed off to his own barn he asked, "Will you be going out on the trail tomorrow? I don't have to go to work until late in the day."

"What time can you be here, Cilla?" I asked. "It's Sunday, so Dad will be at the club early."

"Probably around ten-thirty, she said." We can be ready by eleven-thirty, that work for you, Pete?"

"Perfect." I'll ride over and meet you here."

"Bring a sandwich and we'll have lunch here after we ride," I added.

"OK. See you tomorrow."

When I put Moonbeam away in his stall, I made sure he had a large ration of carrots in appreciation of how perfect he had been on the trail.

Chapter 17

Sunday dawned with gray clouds scuttling across the skies. My first thought was *Oh no—please don't rain.* Dad would still go to the club, golfers, it seemed played in any weather. But riding in the rain was another issue. I knew I would have to assure my mother that I wouldn't ride in the rain to get out of the house with my father. I doubted that Pete would ride in the rain either.

The sun began to peak through holes in the gray sky on the way to the club. Things were looking up. I checked the weather on my phone. The report was encouraging-the threat of rain was moving away from the coast, out to sea. Hopefully, by eleven-thirty our ride would be with the sun shining and Pete on deck.

I daydreamed about the upcoming ride on the way to the barn. Even though Pete had come by the barn when I could only ride in the ring, it hadn't been very often. Not nearly as often as I would have liked. I thought about what it would be like to have some one-on-one time with him. Not that I was at all sure what I would do or say if we ever were alone! *Maybe Wednesday,* I thought. *Depending on when Pete had to work. Cilla was unable to come to the barn on Wednesdays, so no chaperone. Nice thought,* but I knew Warren wasn't about to let me ride on the trail with just Pete. Even if Warren had known Pete better, he still would not have let me ride alone with a boy, out of sight of the barn. Warren and Hazel kept a close eye on us kids, mostly to keep us safe, but also to keep us out of trouble.

The morning dragged on toward eleven-thirty. The good thing was the skies continued to clear. By eleven, the sun was out with only a few remaining gray puffs scuttling by to remind you of the early morning threat. Cilla arrived about ten-thirty. It was early to get the horses ready but we took them out of their stalls to be groomed anyway.

"Did you say anything to your folks about your ride yesterday?" Cilla asked, while we curried and brushed the horses until their coats were clean and gleaming.

"Of course not. How could I? I've never said anything to them about being scared in the first place."

"Pete was sure pleased to see you on the trail again when we met him. Guess he missed you."

"Cilla! He's just a friend. Of course, he was happy that I wasn't grounded anymore," I sputtered.

"Yeah, sure," she drawled, "and speak of the devil, look who just rode in early. Not that he's anxious or anything," she added struggling not to laugh.

Pete saw me in the aisle as he dismounted with that fluid grace he had, and stepped through the huge main doors of the barn. We had put the horses on the cross ties of the main aisle of the barn, Moonbeam first with Peso behind him.

"Hi Katlyn," he said, and a second later when he realized Cilla was just behind me, "Cilla. Looks like we lucked out with the weather and can have our ride after-all. Where should we go today?"

"It doesn't matter to me," I said, hoping that Cilla would volunteer trails that would be closed in.

"How about the short loop to the main loop, maybe twice around the main loop before heading back?" she said. I could have hugged her! She knew that I would feel secure taking the same trails we had taken yesterday.

"Sounds great. You about ready?" he asked.

"All set," Cilla and I chorused.

We headed out across the street as Cilla and I had done yesterday. With the gray skies, none of the golfers had started with an early tee time. No one had, as yet, reached the eighth hole so the coast was clear. Along the fairway, the trail was wide enough that Pete rode alongside me. Upon entering the woods, Pete dropped behind.

"Ready to trot?" called out Cilla. Yesterday I had said "just a jog". Today, with the added security of Pete behind me as well as Cilla in front, I said nothing. Gripping the bucking strap at the front of my saddle to steady my hands, I took a deep breath and managed to allow Moonbeam to pick up a trot behind Peso. *Concentrate on posting*, I told myself. *Hips forward, land in the center of the saddle, hips forward—.* Before I knew it, Cilla called out "walk" and Moonbeam obediently settled into a calm walk.

Cilla turned in the saddle. " Everyone OK back there," she asked. She deliberately did not address me—we both knew she meant just me. Yesterday I had jogged, today I had ridden a working trot. And I was fine!

When we reached parts of the trail suitable to canter but Cilla kept to a walk, Pete took advantage of the opportunities of the wider trail. He came up from behind and rode beside me. We chatted about every-day things. It was enough that we both were doing what we loved and enjoying it together.

"Cilla," I said as we came to a wide stretch of the main loop, "let me come up beside you to trot here. Peso won't try to race Moonbeam and Moonie wouldn't know how to race."

Cilla looked at me, asking with her eyes, *are you sure?* I wasn't sure, to be honest, but I needed to try to trot without being "sandwiched'.

"Besides, I added, moving Moonbeam up beside her, "you have been riding alone without anyone to talk to easily. You need company."

Organizing myself and hoping that Cilla knew enough to grab my reins if needed, I said "Ready, let's go" and urged Moonbeam into a trot. Cilla was careful to stay close to Moonbeam, prepared for any emergency. None arose. It wasn't a long stretch of trail before it narrowed again, but enough that I felt a sense of accomplishment. I trotted on a trail with no one in front of me!

Cilla flashed me a bit grin as she resumed her place as leader. She understood the moment even if she didn't 'whoop and holler' since Pete was there.

It's such a good ride, Katlyn thought as they neared the barn, *I don't want it to be over. But, Pete is staying to have lunch with us. And Cilla's mom is picking her up early again. Maybe Pete can stay a while after Cilla leaves. Wouldn't that be nice!*

Back at the barn, we untacked the horses and put Pete's horse in an empty stall. None of the other kids were at the barn today, so we had the rec room to ourselves.

"Looks like I might be seeing you, ladies, a bit more often now," Pete said after we sat down with our lunches.

"How come?" Cilla asked.

"I've finally landed a job here at the club with the greens-keeper. It will only be part-time for a while because I'll still work at my dad's store. Once I have enough money saved for school, then I'll do school and the store in the winter and then just the club at the end of school."

"I didn't know you were thinking about a club job. I could have asked my father to help you." Katlyn volunteered.

"That's alright. During the years I caddied at the club, I've gotten to know Henry, the greens-keeper, pretty well. I had told him that my real interest was in learning how to do what he did. He told me about the courses I should take but said on-the-job-training was valuable too. As soon as there was an opening at the club, he offered to let me know. And he did."

"I must admit I know nothing about a golf course, except to stay off greens and out of sand traps, but my father says that this course is one of the top courses in the country. I would think that would make it one of best places to learn how to maintain a course." Katlyn offered.

"What will you be doing?" chimed in Cilla.

"Guess what? The first job is to learn about the machinery, what it's used for and how to maintain it. So, for the first couple of weeks, I'll be right here at the barn. Well, almost right here-just out the driveway in back at the maintenance sheds."

The thought blossomed in Katlyn's mind—Wednesdays could become wonderful days for the next several weeks.

"After you learn the machinery and stuff, what happens?" Katlyn asked, trying to be subtle about how long 'good Wednesdays' might last.

From then on, you are mostly out on the course. You graduate to playing with the big fairway mowers and the other equipment. Once you know about the practical stuff, then it's time for college courses for the theoretical and technical knowledge needed to manage the grounds of a club.

So, not too many whole days, but maybe some free lunch-times, Katlyn thought.

"I've got to go or I'll be late for my shift at the store. See you ladies Wednesday, perhaps? inquired Pete.

"Not me," said Cilla "but Katlyn's usually here on Wednesdays."

"OK, see you then, Katlyn."

As soon as Pete left, Cilla turned to Katlyn, "How about that Miss Katlyn! Right here in our own backyard, so to speak. For 'several weeks' at least. Isn't it lucky that you always get to stay later on Wednesdays?"

"Cilla, I don't know what you're talking about, you're just being silly," Katlyn said, trying in vain not to blush.

"Oh, sure, you have no idea what I mean. Then, how come your cheeks are pinker than a flamingo? she teased.

I gave a sigh of relief when her mother's arrival ended the conversation. Cilla couldn't resist a parting volley; "have fun Wednesday. I'll call you. See you Saturday." And was out the door.

Chapter 18

Over the next several days, Katlyn gave thought off and on to what changes the new proximity to Pete might bring. The maintenance sheds, although just on the other side of the back driveway, might as well have been across an ocean. The riders and greens-keeping staff sailed this ocean as their highway. They would acknowledge the other when passing, but each never made port on the other side.

She could not enter the maintenance world, Pete, however, was now of both worlds. She wondered if he would take his lunch breaks with her, as he had said. She hoped he had meant it.

After helping with chores around the barn Wednesday morning, Katlyn tacked up Moonbeam and went to the ring.

"Ok, Moonbeam, today we work on the requirements of the Road Hack class." Katlyn wasn't sure whether she was giving Moonbeam fair warning or trying to convince herself that she could accomplish this goal. After letting him warm-up at a walk, Katlyn ordered, "trot, Moonie".

This is fine, Katlyn muttered to herself, *a steady working trot and my hands on the reins are almost at the buckle. Now across a short diagonal into a lengthening.* A few strides were enough to have Katlyn grabbing to shorten her reins as quickly as possible to regain control.

Katlyn reestablished her position, lost as Moonbeam had increased his speed across the diagonal. While she walked Moonbeam and worked to get her breathing to return to normal, she thought about what had just taken place. *Moonbeam had thought, apparently, that when I urged him to be more forward, it meant to go faster. With little or no contact because of the loose rein, I couldn't or didn't show him that wasn't what I wanted. When I lost my position and balance, it confused and unbalanced him, so he had gone faster, trying to regain his own balance.*

Well, she reasoned, *maybe this needs to be a two-step process. First, he needs to learn to go bigger, not faster. Then, I must get control of myself to ride the bigger stride, even on a loose rein, without panicking. That is obviously going to be easier said than done if what we just did is any indication!*

Moonbeam was a smart horse with a good foundation of skills. With the security of shorter reins and more control, Moonbeam quickly figured out what I was asking of him, he needed to produce power not speed.

Ok, I thought, *now it's my turn. I can ride it when I have control with a shorter rein, can I still ride it on a longer rein?*

If I start the diagonal after THAT CORNER, I won't have to see the raw wood. She put Moonbeam into a trot with a long rein, made a big circle ensuring they both were organized, and after *that* corner, headed him across the diagonal, asking for the lengthened stride. Moonbeam, showing off that he had learned this lesson, responded on cue. After the initial stride, Katlyn felt her body respond to her memories, not her hopes. becoming tense and stiff. Tears flowing, she pulled Moonbeam to a walk. She glanced over at Warren. He was concentrating on the youngster he was teaching so didn't notice her tears. Katlyn patted Moonbeam as she left the ring, her thoughts in a turmoil. *He was so good and I was so awful. Am I ever going to be able to get over this?* she asked herself.

There was nobody around to notice how depressed Katlyn was as she went about untacking Moonbeam and putting him in his stall. She retreated to the rec room. *Thank goodness no one is here. I don't think I could bear to see anyone right now,* she thought, plunking herself down on the couch.

A few minutes later, the door opened. It was Pete. Katlyn in her misery had completely forgotten they were to have lunch today.

Pete took one look at Katlyn, dropped his lunch on the table as he went by and sat beside her on the couch.

"What's the matter? You look awful. What happened? Did Moonbeam throw you?" The questions came too fast to answer.

It needed only the concern in his voice for Katlyn's eyes to start to fill again.

"Oh, Pete, I am so discouraged! I'm almost ready to give it all up."

Pete put his arm around her should and pulled her closer to him. "Katlyn, you don't mean that. You know you don't. Tell me what happened."

Katlyn told him about the events of the morning's ride. *Sitting there on the couch with Pete's arm around me makes my ride much less terrible and important,* she realized. She turned to Pete as she finished, He looked at her as if for permission, and seeing no refusal, gently kissed her.

Katlyn was surprised, confused, uncertain what to do, then responding to her feelings, kissed him back. After a few moments of neither one seeming to know what to do next, other than savor what had just happened, Pete got up and went to the table.

"We had better eat or I'll be due back at the job and still be hungry."

"You're right," Katlyn replied, glad to act as if nothing had happened.

As they ate, she and Pete talked about the next steps that Katlyn might try in her training for the road hack class.

"You might try riding the first part of the diagonal with the usual contact," Pete suggested, "then in the middle part let the reins go longer for a few strides, but pick up the contact again for the last part as you prepare the transition to the working trot."

"That sounds like it would work, both for Moonbeam and for me. Eventually, I would hope that the middle part, with the rein long, can be more and more of the diagonal."

Pete got up to leave. At the door, as if to acknowledge their changed relationship, he put his arms around Katlyn gave her a quick hug and a kiss on the cheek, said, "I'll see you Saturday," and left.

Katlyn sat at the table again, nursing the remains of her coke. She had a lot of feelings to sort out. *That was some lunch,* she thought. *Maybe when I figure out what happened, I'll talk to Cilla about it. One thing is for sure, it was very nice!*

Cilla called that night, "Well, how did it go? How was he now that you had a chance to be alone with him?"

"It was fine," Katlyn replied. "I had a really bad ride with Moonbeam before lunch and Pete had a good suggestion of something to try to make it better. We had lunch and then he had to go back to work."

"That's all?" asked Cilla in a tone of voice that said she didn't believe a word that I said.

"Pretty much. I can't wait to see if his suggestion works, though." Katlyn knew that Cilla was disappointed by here responses. *I can't talk about it yet, even to Cilla,* she thought. *Maybe by Saturday, I'll have sorted it out and can tell her about it then.* "Anyway, I'll see you Saturday. You still ok to spend the night here?" she asked.

"Yes, everything is still on. Are we still going to the beach in the afternoon?"

"Yes, that's the plan. Patty will be with us and her father is going to man the grill for a cookout for supper. Some of the other kids in the neighborhood will be at the barbeque too. Patty's bringing an air mattress to sleep on since my room only has two bed and they're twins. Well, I have to go. See you then."

Chapter 19

The next two days were busy ones with the Sheffield boys. The weather was off and on cloudy, drizzling and outright rain. Keeping the boys occupied since we couldn't go to the beach, was a full-time job. There were just enough no-actual-rain times that I could take them outside to burn off some of their energy.

Saturday finally came. I doublechecked the schedule with Mom. " I'm going to the barn with Dad this morning, but you are going to come pick up Cilla and me at the barn about twelve thirty, right? Then Cilla, Patty and I are going to the beach. We'll take our bikes. Cilla can use William's. After Mr. DeLong's barbeque, Patty and Cilla are spending the night. Cilla will go to the barn with me in the morning and her mother will pick her up there after we ride."

"That's what I understand," said Mom. "By the way, where is Patty going to sleep?"

"She's bringing an air mattress over. One of us will sleep on that."

"Good. I'll see you about twelve thirty at the barn."

Katlyn ambled down the ninth, enjoying the beginnings of a beautiful day after two days of rain. Further down the fairway, she noticed one of the mowers stopped in the thick rough of the fairway with a maintenance cart pulled up beside it. As she got closer, she recognized Pete with one of the mowing men. Much as she would have liked to stop and talk to him, she knew she couldn't. She settled for a distant "Hi" and a casual wave and kept on walking down the fairway.

As she neared the end of the fairway, she heard the maintenance cart coming up behind her. It stopped. "Hop in," said Pete," I'll give you a lift the rest of the way."

He reached the passenger side to give her a hand into the cart. Katlyn settled into the seat, but Pete didn't release her hand. "Hi," he said softly, looking directly at her. Katlyn paused, surprised that he still held her hand, then responded shyly, "Hi yourself."

Pete continued as if nothing was happening, even though he still held her hand as he drove, "I won't make it for lunch today. With the rain, the mowers are having a tough time dealing with the high, wet rough of the fairways. I'll be in and out all day keeping the machines running. If I can, I'll take a quick break to see how you do with Moonbeam."

"That would be great. I'm going to work him in the ring just long enough to remind him of Wednesday's lesson and to try your suggestion. Then Cilla and I are going out on the trail. I'll probably be in the ring about nine-thirty, quarter to ten."

"Cilla," Katlyn said when she was ready to mount up, "I am going to ride in the ring just long enough to remind Moonbeam of how to lengthen his trot and try Pete's suggestion. Then we can go on the trail. OK?"

"Sure, that's fine. Peso can use a little 'tuning-up' too. I haven't schooled him in a while."

After the warm-up, Katlyn asked Moonbeam for a lengthened trot across the diagonal, counting the strides. It was fifteen strides. *If I try a looser rein after five strides, go five strides and then retake the contact for the remaining five, that should work*, she told herself. *If I can keep the panic at bay for five strides!*

Katlyn planned to use the same diagonal Moonbeam was accustomed to, with the ugly raw wood of the repaired boards at her back. First making sure she had a rhythmic working trot Katlyn, Katlyn asked Moonbeam for a big circle and as she finished the circle, straightened him onto a long diagonal across the ring.

One, two, three, four, get ready, five, give some rein she told herself. *One, Moonbeam didn't break or go faster, just bigger, two,* Katlyn felt her throat tightening, *three,* she recognized that the muscles of her body were starting to stiffen, *four, get ready to take back the contact, five, shorten the reins,* Katlyn felt her throat relax and took a deep breath, finished the diagonal, and came to a working trot, then walk.

"That was great," Pete said." I could see you start to get tense, but you didn't have enough time to have a melt-down before you took the reins again."

Katlyn was surprised to hear his voice. She had been so concentrated on counting strides and loosening her contact, she had not noticed that he was leaning on the ring fence to watch. She walked Moonbeam over to him. "That was such a terrific suggestion! And it worked! I was so busy counting, my mind had a hard time thinking of anything else. I can't thank you enough."

"No thanks required," said Pete. "I'm glad it worked. You will be doing the entire diagonal on a loose rein in no time. Now, I have to get back to work," he continued. His expression said that was not his first choice of what he would like to be doing. "Have a good ride, Katlyn. See you tomorrow, Cilla."

As Pete headed back to the maintenance shed, Katlyn came alongside Cilla. "Ready to go out?" she asked. "As always," quipped Cilla and led the way to the trail.

The rest of the day flew by. Mrs. Lange picked them up, they had a quick lunch at Katlyn's house and were on their way to an afternoon at the beach.

Katlyn explained to Cilla. "It's only a short bike ride to the beach. The last stretch of it is exhilarating. Just before the beach, you are at the top of a steep hill. After you have swooped down the hill, you cross the beach road, and you're there, at the cut onto the beach itself. I have to admit, though, that hill isn't nearly as much fun on the way home. After a couple of hours on the beach, I barely have the energy to walk my bike up it, never mind try to pedal up it!"

By the time they returned home, surfeited with sun and sea, it was time for showers and to get dressed for the barbeque.

Later, after a fun barbeque, they changed into pj's, ready for bed. They retrieved a large bowl of popcorn Mrs. Lange had fixed for them, raided the fridge for cold drinks, and retreated to Katlyn's room. They settled down on Patty's air mattress, taking up the space between the twin beds, in front of the fireplace in Katlyn's room. Katlyn loved having a fire during the winter months.

As soon as they were settled, Cilla announced, "Katlyn, no more stalling. Tell us about Wednesday. What's going on with Pete? I know something is, if only because you haven't said a word about it. So-o-o, tell all!"

"I agree with Cilla" chimed in Patty. "You're hiding something. Come-on, we wouldn't say anything to anyone else, you know that."

"I wasn't hiding anything," answered Katlyn after a pause. I just didn't know what to say. And I wasn't sure about what my feelings were, so I couldn't talk about it, even to you two."

"What was there that was so hard to say?" asked Patty.

"Well, sort of the whole thing."

"Wait a minute," said Cilla. "I don't understand. What is 'the whole thing'? Maybe you better start at the beginning."

"OK. Well, I had been trying to school Moonbeam and it was terrible. I was really upset and discouraged. I went into the rec room to avoid everyone, so they wouldn't see I had been crying. I had stopped the tears and was just sitting there when Pete came in.

"I was so upset, I had completely forgotten about having lunch with him. He took one look at me, asked what had happened, and before I knew it he was on the couch beside me with his arm around my shoulder, snuggling me next to him. He was so concerned, my eyes started to fill again.

"As I turned to him to say something, he just looked at me for a moment and...

and... then he kissed me," she blurted out.

"And then? What did you do?" asked Patty.

"For a second or so I didn't do anything, I was so surprised. Plus, I didn't know what to do. Then I decided it was fine, so I kissed him back. He still had his arm around me. I wasn't anxious to end that so we just sat there for a few minutes. Then we got up, sat at the table to eat and talked about what could be done to change the disaster of the morning.

"Before he left, he hugged me and gave me a kiss on the cheek. I just stood there, like a ninny, trying to figure out what had just happened. Whatever it was, I knew I liked it."

"Wow, what's not to like," said Cilla "But why so confused? I've told you from the beginning when we first met him, he likes you. He's a nice guy and he's only a couple of years older than you. You are old enough to have a boyfriend, so what's the problem?"

"I don't know. I don't know what comes next, what to do. I've never had a boyfriend that I felt this way about. I would really like to be with him more, but I know that isn't going to be possible."

"What do you mean?" Cilla and Patty said at the same time.

"Well, once school starts again, I can only be here weekends. Pete will still be working for his father, and for Henry here at the club, and he will have started taking some courses. How much time is he going to have to ride? Not much, I would guess.

"Since he drives, I suppose he could come pick me up to go out to the movies or something, or there might be some things at school I would be able to invite him to but that isn't going to happen. Once my mother finds out about him, she will have a fit. A Townie, who indirectly works for my father, since he is Henry's boss? Not a snowflake's chance in H— she would allow me to go out with him. Remember, she is firmly of the belief that you can't marry someone you have never met!"

"I don't like to say it, but I have to agree with you, Katlyn. Your mother holds some strong views. I've never met Pete as you have Cilla, but I have known Katlyn's mom for a long time. I think she is right. Pete would not go over big with Mrs. Lange."

"Well, you can at least enjoy it while it lasts," added the ever-optimistic Cilla. "By the end of the summer, you might wonder what you saw in each other anyway. You should see him, Patty. He is really cute."

Settled in bed with the lights out, Katlyn fell asleep with the thoughts *Cilla is right. Pete is cute …and nice …and caring…. and ,*

Chapter 20

On the way to the stables the following morning, Katlyn said, "Cilla, do you mind if I volunteer your services to Warren?"

"About what?" she asked.

"Well, about fence of the ring. Every time I look at that raw wood, I see myself crashing through it. It's been fixed long enough for it to be painted. I think Warren was holding off until closer to the show and then give the entire ring fence a coat of paint. But I was thinking that if I didn't have to look at that raw wood every time I came around that corner, maybe I could stay more relaxed and focused. If I volunteered to paint it, would you help?"

"Sure, why not. With two of us, it wouldn't take very long. Maybe some of the other kids would help too. We could be like Tom Sawyer and charge them for the privilege!"

"I doubt that would fly in today's world," laughed Katlyn. "I'll ask Warren."

She tracked down Warren in the barn and told him about her suggestion.

"Fine, Katlyn, if you are sure you want to take on such a project. I'll have the paint and brushes ready when you come next weekend. It would be a big help-one less thing for me to get done before the show."

Katlyn was torn about seeing Pete. now that Cilla knew about Wednesday's lunch with Pete. She hoped to see him, but also hoped not to see him. In the presence of Cilla, she was uncertain how to act around him. *If we have lunch together, what if he holds my hand or gives me a hug. Cilla will see it,* she thought. *I'll be embarrassed, even though I want him to do just that, give me a hug and hold my hand!*

Cilla and Katlyn were just finishing tacking up the horses when Katlyn's worries were resolved. Pete cane riding into the yard on Scout.

"Hi ladies. I only have the morning off so I thought I would stop by to see if you were available for a trail ride."

"Your timing is perfect" Cilla responded. "We are just about to go out."

Cilla led Peso to the mounting block and mounted. Katlyn followed quickly with Moonbeam. Cilla led the way to the trail out the back driveway. Katlyn, drawn like a magnet, fell in beside Scout following Cilla. Kate was grateful that Cilla couldn't see the immediate touch of hands of the riders behind her.

They had a fun run ride, joking and teasing each other., enjoying the sunshine and tranquility of the woods. There were even a few moments of seriousness.

"There's a nice stretch of trail for trotting coming up. Want to try the extended trot Katlyn?" asked Pete. "Cilla will set the pace in front and with me behind you, you will be safely sandwiched in while you try a few strides on a loose rein. After all, the Road Hack class is supposed to showcase trail riding manners., isn't it?"

Katlyn thought I won't be able to live with myself if I disappoint Pete's expectations and say no to this. Trying to sound aa great deal more confident than she felt, she said, "Ok, Pete. I think that I can manage that. Moonbeam has been so good in the ring with extending the trot without rushing, I am sure that he will do the same on the trail."

"We're here," Cilla said. "A short bit of working trot, then a short spurt of extended and back to working-OK?" she asked.

Nobody objecting, she urged Peso into a smooth working trot, Moonbeam obediently following Peso's lead. When Cilla ordered "extend", Katlyn reminded herself to start her silent litany.

"One, let the rein go long, two, deep breath, three, let the reins stay long, four, five, softly on the longer rein, deep breath again, six, start to take contact again, slowly, six, relax, ride the big trot, with some contact and make the transitions to the working trot and walk"

Pete came up beside Moonbeam. He reached across and gave her a half hug. "You and Moonbeam were super," he said.

Katlyn was so relieved that she had managed the extended trot, happy that she has not disappointed Pete, and delighted that he hugged her, she forgot all about being embarrassed that Cilla saw him hug her.

"That was real progress, Katlyn," Cilla added. Katlyn couldn't tell from the teasing smile on her face whether she meant the extended trot or that Cilla was now privy to Pete's display of affection. They headed for the barn at a leisurely walk, letting the horses cool down. Pete turned off to go to his own barn.

"I won't see you tomorrow," he said, "I have a killer work schedule. "But, Wednesday?" he asked, looking at Katlyn.

"I'll be here. Moonie and I still have a lot of ground to cover before we will be even close to ready for the show."

"See you then," he said.

As they continued toward their barn, Cilla said," You rode that extended trot just right, Katlyn. Even though I couldn't see it, I could hear you behind me and hear the beat of Moonbeam's footfalls. They were in the same rhythm as those of Peso. I couldn't tell if you had a loose rein but from Pete's reaction I guess that you managed that as well."

"I wasn't at all sure that I could let go enough for a loose rein on the trail, even for a few strides, but between you and Pete, I somehow was able to manage it.

"You did, and that's progress."

"I appreciate all the help you have given me, Cilla. Really, I mean it." Katlyn added. "It's made a big difference."

Warren greeted them when they arrived at the barn. "I hope you two have your painting clothes handy. The paint and brushes are here, ready for you to go to work."

"Ok, we're almost ready. We just have to put the horses away and grab some lunch. Then we will be on the clock, so to speak." Katlyn said. "After lunch, we'll see if Jake and any of the others want to join in."

Jake joined us part-way through lunch and agreed to join the 'paint group'.

By the time the paint was stirred, poured into smaller buckets for each painter and they moved to the ring, "Katlyn said to the others, "We have the makings of a party."

She continued, "I'm going to start at the repaired part of the fence, my very own bête noire. Besides, the raw wood is going to need more coats of paint than the rest of the fence."

"You start on the outside, I do the inside," said Cilla. It will go faster that way. After a few moments, Katlyn looked at Cilla and laughed. "It's a good thing we put these plastic garbage bags on. My clothes would sure be a mess from your splashes without it."

"Mine too," she replied. "But, it does go much faster with someone on each side."

After an hour or so of painting, Katlyn said to everyone, "That's enough for one day. Let's get cleaned up and have a cold drink. We covered nearly half of the ring today, which is enough for one day."

Divesting themselves of the paint-splattered garbage bags, without adding more paint to their person, proved a challenge. Particularly as the hose used to wash off paint was as often 'misdirected' to someone else's body-part where the paint was conspicuous by its absence. Eventually, the mission was accomplished.

Cilla, Katlyn, Jake and the others repaired to the rec room for well-deserved cold drinks, Katlyn looked at the repaired section. *Good,* she thought. *Even covered with only one coat of paint, it almost blends with the remaining fence. A slight shadow still shows, but it doesn't jump out and bite you as it had. Now maybe I can ignore it!*

Chapter 21

Will this day never end! thought Katlyn. Monday had arrived with an overcast dull, gray sky. It didn't so much promise rain as it denied sunshine. She and the Sheffield boys walked to the beach. It wasn't a good day to go in the water but, searching the rock pools for minnows and crabs was better than being cooped up in the house. And, on the beach, they could burn off some energy chasing the waves.

Tuesday dawned with another dreary start to the day. By mid-morning, it was raining. Housebound, keeping the boys occupied was a challenge. Although with each hour that passed, Katlyn thought, *one hour closed to Wednesday. Please, please let the rain stop by the morning. I'll only be riding in the ring anyway, so even if the woods are still wet, it won't matter. And the footing in the ring dries out quickly.*

Although she couldn't wait for it to arrive, Katlyn was conflicted about Wednesday. She looked forward to being with Pete again, whether it could only be a short break or if they were lucky, an entire lunch hour. But, with no chaperone! She was also anxious to discover if she could give Moonbeam a loose rein for an additional number of strides of extended trot. On the trail, it had gone well. Now, could she do it alone, not sandwiched between Cilla and Pete?

Wednesday greeted Katlyn with the sun shining through her window behind the headboard of her bed. Her prayers were answered. It would be a barn day. More importantly, it would be a Pete day. Katlyn rummaged around in her shirt drawer to find a blue shirt to wear after she rode. She was in luck, there were two clean ones. She tucked one in her carry-all and put on the other. *Blue coordinate with my jodhpurs,* she thought, *but it also makes my eyes look very blue.* She laughed at herself. *Look at me, thinking about how I look-which color shirt makes my eyes pretty! Will he get close enough to see the color of my eyes?* she wondered.

In the summertime, when her father left for the club so early, Katlyn's mother often did not get up with them. Her father was not one to notice the care with which Katlyn had dressed that morning. Her mother surely would have, but Katlyn was spared her observing eye this morning.

Katlyn always enjoyed the walk down the ninth to the barn. The dew was still on the grass, the sun just rising over the tops of the tall pines which bordered the road side of the fairway. It was very quiet, only the soft murmur of a gang mower on a distant fairway to intrude on the silence of the early morning. As she walked along, Kathlyn planned her ride with Moonbeam. Her planning kept getting interrupted by thoughts of Pete. *Would they be able to have lunch? What would they talk about? Would he kiss her again? (definitely a most important consideration.) If he did, what should she do, if anything?*

When she arrived at the barn, Katlyn helped out with the remaining morning chores, then brought Moonbeam out from his stall. As she curried and brushed him, she reviewed her approach to today's schooling. Her main goal was to add more strides on a loose rein, to the extended trot. Without Cilla in front to block any speed-up, it was a scary thought.

After a warm-up period, Katlyn started to school the extended trot. The five-stride exercise that she and Moonbeam had worked on, was OK. *Not great,* she said to herself, *but passable. Now for the hard part. I've managed five, can I do eight? Just three more strides before taking the rein again? Only two regular strides, then loosen, keep going for the count of eight, then take contact and transition down.*

She gathered her courage, put Moonie into a trot circle and started across the diagonal. *One, two, three— loosen the rein! Keep counting, four— I can't breathe, five— I'm folding in the middle, six—my hands are like iron fists. That's it—back with the reins! Bad transition, but Moonie stopped.*

Katlyn was disgusted with herself. *One lousy step more before I panicked. And even counting, I still lost it! At the rate of one additional step each schooling session, I'll be old and gray before we are able to extend the entire diagonal!*

But, as she walked Moonbeam and regrouped, she consoled herself with the fact she did manage one more stride before her fear caught up with her. Then a surprising realization-she was more disgusted with herself then scared after the diagonal. *Maybe that is a kind of progress too,* she thought.

"OK, let's try it a different way. Maybe it will be better," she said to Moonbeam as if he was following her thinking. "It would be hard to be worse", she muttered as she collected her reins to trot. Heading down the long side of the ring, Katlyn counted aloud, "one, two, three, loosen, *keep counting,* four, *breathe,* five— *I'm folding in the middle— that's OK—now gather the reins,* one, two, transition! She was amazed. Hearing her own voice doing the counting so distracted her, she had just ridden the exercise. She had ignored completely the bigger stride that Moonbeam had given her. She smiled when she thought of what someone must think, had they been around to hear her crazy out-loud counting. But, no one had been in the ring, so she was safe on that score.

Encouraged, Katlyn did the exercise again, with the same good results. She decided to push herself. "Let's try for five, Moonie" she said. Nearly yelling the count with enthusiasm this time, they accomplished the five strides, without a huge intake of breath needed at the end of the fifth stride. Katlyn congratulated herself when she realized that she also had not stopped breathing normally at all.

Arms around Moonie's neck she said, "You are a super boy. That's enough work for one day." They walked to the barn, each well pleased with their performance of the day.

Katlyn had just finished closing the tabs on Moonbeam's fly mask when the stall door opened behind her.

"Hi there," said Pete. He took her hand, led her to the back corner of the stall, drew her into his arms and kissed her. "Hi again," he said as he held her close.

Katlyn rested against him briefly, then reached up and kissed him. "Hi yourself" she whispered. Moonbeam, engrossed in his mid-day hay, ignored them. They broke apart at the sound of footsteps in the aisle and left Moonbeam to his lunch.

"Sorry I didn't get to see your ride," Pete said, as they walked hand in hand to the rec room. "How did it go?"

"Some good, some not so good. But over-all, I think some minor improvements. What about you, still repairing equipment?"

"Nope, I just got promoted. Now I get to play with the gang mowers out in the fresh air. Staying inside is not my thing. If I could stand to be inside all the time, I'd stay working for my father.

Pete continued, "The thing about the mowing is that it's not just mindlessly running the mowers over the grass. Well, I mean, it could be, I suppose. But Henry is teaching me the how's and why's of which parts of the fairways need to be what length. It's really interesting."

Pete opened the door to the rec room and Katlyn went to put her lunch on the table. Instead of following suit, Pete headed for the couch and dropped his brown bag there, as he went to the coke machine. Katlyn changed direction mid-stride to also drop her lunch on the couch, then also headed to get a drink.

Sitting close to each other on the couch, Katlyn described her ride. "One thing," she said" Now that part of the fence is painted, I wasn't reminded every time I came around that corner. It's a lot easier to keep my concentration without that raw wound staring at me each time around."

They continued to talk about everything and nothing until it was time for Pete to get back to work. Still thankfully alone, Pete embraced Katlyn before leaving, gave her a lingering parting kiss and was out the door.

And, thought Katlyn, *that will have to* do, *probably until next Wednesday, a whole week away!*

Chapter 22

When Cilla arrived at the barn the following Saturday, Katlyn said," Let's just trail ride today. Moonbeam has been schooling hard, he and I need a break. Just a fun day. It's a perfect day for it."

"Sounds like a wonderful idea. Lunch at the orchard? Cilla asked.

"Sure, why not. Add the saddlebags behind your saddle. I'll put a blanket on mine. I'll get my lunch."

Once organized for their picnic, they were ready to head out to their favorite spot. *A very favorite spot* thought Katlyn, *I met Pete there.*

Moonbeam had two days off but is happy to amble along and be perfect. Walking and trotting with Cilla in the lead, are fine with Katlyn. She even manages a few trot strides on a loose contact rein. Mostly Katlyn and Cilla just talk and fill each other in on their week. Cilla, of course, must have every detail about Wednesday with Pete. Katlyn had already filled her in when they spoke on the phone Wednesday evening, but Cilla pushed for each and every detail of Katlyn's time with Pete.

They reach the two adjoining grassy fields, full of sunlight, where the path nestles beside the moss and lichen covered stone wall bordering the road. The buzz of grasshoppers feasting in the sunlit fields assaults the riders after the quiet of the woods. At the far edge of the second field, the undergrowth and trees reclaimed their domain and the path ends to cross the road and pick up again on the other side.

Let's just keep it to a trot, Kaitlyn thinks as they reach this spot where they usually canter, but before she can say anything, Cilia urges her horse into a full canter. Moonbeam follows without hesitation.

Katlyn gasped, started to panic and then worked to get control of herself. She bridged her reins and settled into a strong two-point position. She thought, *Enough of being afraid! I must let him canter. I just must!* Out of nowhere, the picture of a little blue steam engine popped into her mind. The refrain *I think I can, I think I can echoed in her mind in rhythm with the beat of the canter.* Gone was the terrifying vision of the barred gate rushing toward her., Before she knew it, she had caught up with Cilla, waiting for her at the end of the second field.

Laughing, almost crying. Cilla says "You did it! You cantered without freezing up! Hurray! You OK?"

"If you had told me you were going to canter, I would have 'said don't you dare'," said Katlyn, trying to sound angry but failing. "But then, Moonbeam was cantering and somehow this time, I knew I had to let him canter. After a few strides, it suddenly seemed OK, just a canter." Katlyn couldn't admit the refrain of the kid's story which had repeated over and over in her head.

As they crossed the road and entered the woods again, Katlyn pondered what had just happened. *What had just taken place?* she thought. Katlyn was very quiet until they reached the orchard.

They headed off the trail toward one of the large trees that dotted the side of the hill, between the orchard and the road. Katlyn spread the blanket in the shade of the tree while Cilla removed bridles and put halters on the horses so they could graze while they ate.

Settled with their lunches Cilla said, "What's going on, Katlyn? You haven't said two words since the fields. How come? Are you mad at me for cantering without warning you?"

"No, of course not. I told you, it was OK. In fact, more than OK. I have been trying to figure out what happened, what was different. Why was it suddenly just a canter?

"Cilla, let me ask you something" ventured Katlyn. "Do you think that I could be my own worst enemy? That so long as all I could see was that barred gate coming at me, I couldn't make use of any of the skills that I have had for years?"

"Uh, I don't know for sure," replied Cilla" but I think it must be something like that. You haven't used your hands to stop a horse for years. Then, after Socks bolted, it was as if using your hands was the only thing you could do and of course, it didn't work, it only made things worse."

"It was as if I had a video set to a continuous replay of the barred gate rushing toward me and the crash through the fence and the play button was pushed the minute I asked the horse for anything faster than a walk."

"Then what was different when you cantered in the fields? Cilla asked.

"I'm not sure. I think partly it was because I didn't have any warning of the canter. Does that make sense?"

"If you mean that you didn't have time to think about it and push your 'play' button, then, yes it does." offered Cilla.

"That's what I mean. I was so busy staying on and riding the canter, I didn't have time to think of anything else." Katlyn hesitated, then added,

"And … you know that kid's book we all read? About Thomas, the little engine that could? I know it sounds silly but as I settled into my two point, suddenly the picture of that little engine hauling a long line of freight cars up that steep incline and puffing 'I think I can, over and over popped into my mine and became one with the beat of the canter. Except then it became, 'I know I can' and by the end of the middle of the second field it was 'I can, I can'. And I could! The old video was gone. Pouf, just gone. Now, something that Warren said a few weeks back makes sense."

"Why? What did he say?"

"He said that I had to recognize the difference between feelings and fact. And when I was worried about what might happen, those negative thoughts were just feelings, not facts and I had to challenge them. When I recognized them as just feelings, not facts, then I could put them aside as of no consequence. I think that's what I just did— with the help of 'the little engine that could'."

"I hope it is gone forever!" said Cilla. But we'll see I suppose. For now, let's get the horses and head back. We can try the canter at the twin fields if you want. It would be a real test, since this time you would know that we are going to canter."

"It may be a bit shaky, but I think that 'video' is gone once and for all. The 'Thomas' video is much more fun" Katlyn joked.

When they reached the twin field, Cilla asked "Ready?"

"Let's go" said Katlyn.

With Cilla in the lead, they picked up the canter. For a second or so, Katlyn realized that she was about to push the old, scary video play button. *No., not that video. Play the one of Thomas,* she said to herself. and broke into Thomas' mantra to match the strides of the canter. It worked. Once again, she could enjoy the easy swinging rhythm of Moonbeam's comfortable canter.

"Wait until you tell Warren, said Cilla. "He'll be so pleased."

"Yeah. And he'll just give me that slow grin of his and say "Well, of course, you could canter, Katlyn. What's the big deal?" as if nothing had ever happened!"

Cilla laughed. "You are so right."

The person Katlyn wanted most to share her news with was Pete. Katlyn wished she had Pete's phone number to tell him about her ride. But she knew even if she had it, she wouldn't call him—what if someone else answered his phone—what would she say? How would she explain why a girl was calling him? What if her mother overheard her and asked about it? She knew her mother well enough to know that if she didn't know anything about Pete, she couldn't have anything to say about the relationship. Maybe, she hoped, he would have some time off on Sunday.

Katlyn was right. Late Sunday morning, Pete came riding up to the barn. Katlyn's first reaction was to go racing up to him to tell him her news but managed to tone it down to a big smile as she stroked his horse while he dismounted.

He asked," why the happy face?" She told him of her ride with Cilla.

"That's wonderful, Katlyn," and he gave her a big hug. Had they been other than in the middle of the yard in front of the barn, Katlyn knew he would have also kissed her, *but not here, with everyone around, thank goodness!* she thought.

Pete couldn't stay long. He was due at his father's store shortly. Cilla, Katlyn, and Pete chatted, caught up with each other's news and then Pete had to leave. Katlyn wished they had had more time to spend with each other, but at least she had a chance to tell him about being able to canter, which was the big thing. She still glowed in his delight of her accomplishment. Anything more would have to wait until Wednesday.

Chapter 23

Wednesday arrived with Katlyn in a new and optimistic frame of mind. She was ready to begin to concentrate Moonbeam's schooling on those requirements of the classes in the Fall show that she had been avoiding. Walking Moonbeam to the ring she talked to him about the 'new start', before Warren joined them for her lesson.

"Here's the deal, Moonie. Since I've accepted responsibility to stop re-living the crash and get on with riding, the Fall show has become more certain, not just a maybe. I know that the requirement for the simple canter lead change in a figure eight has been undoable. I know, it's not your fault. You have been super. But if I can turn off that ancient video, stay centered and relaxed at the canter, you can hear my half-halt and execute the lead change smoothly. OK?"

Whether Moonbeam took her talk to heart or if she had just convinced herself, it didn't matter. She hoped with Warren's help, they each would be ready.

When Warren arrived, he was riding one of the boarder's horses who needed the exercise, but also to implement his goals for the lesson. He called Katlyn to the center of the ring.

"Katlyn, my thoughts about today's lesson; warm-up, then check to be sure that the canter on a loose rein is still OK, and work on the figure eight lead changes for a few times. Mainly, I want to introduce the hand gallop. I doubt that Moonbeam has galloped since he was a two-year-old. Certainly, he hasn't galloped in the five years Mrs. P. has owned him."

The road hack class requirement of a hand gallop had been completely beyond anything Katlyn could contemplate. It made no difference that the gait was ridden with contact of the rein and only a few horses of the class would gallop together. She couldn't envision it happening.

"The first two sound fine," said Katlyn, "I'm not too sure about the hand gallop, but we'll see."

Katlyn asked Moonbeam for a loose rein canter, sure that she could communicate with him, that he would listen to her and the downward transition to trot would be made smoothly and correctly. And it was.

"Let's see the figure eight lead changes," asked Warren.

The first two times were less than great. Moonbeam did them, but not fluidly and with impulsion. Warren made some suggestions about forwardness and Katlyn's balance. After she had made the corrections, the figure improved.

"Now that you know what you need to work on to get those smooth changes, let's think about the hand gallop. You understand that you will have contact with the reins. This part of the class is not on a loose rein. But you will have to gallop with several of the other horses at the same time. Moonbeam is not competitive, so it is unlikely that he will take galloping with several horses as a race. I want you to try it just the length of the long side, then come back to the canter and walk and we'll talk about it. Alright?"

"If you say so," Katlyn said. "Do I go to the gallop from a canter?"

"Yes, start the canter just before the gate and use the corner to leg yield a few strides to set him up in balance. Then ask for a bigger, longer stride. Be sure to give him some rein, even while you maintain contact because he must stretch his neck to balance in the gallop."

"What do you think, Moonbeam," she said, as much to herself as him, "shall we try it?"

Katlyn thought *thank goodness Warren didn't want the gallop until after we are past 'the fateful' corner. Even though it's now painted and just another part of the ring fence, I'd rather be on the safe side and not raise any ghosts.*

Katlyn picked up the canter and concentrated on leg yielding into the corner. Starting down the long side of the ring, she took a deep breath, thought of her friendly little blue puff-a-belly engine, whispered "Let's go Moonie" and urged him forward. Moonbeam initially acted as if he couldn't believe Katlyn wanted him to go faster. As Katlyn remembered to give him some rein and kept urging him forward, he figured out what she wanted. He stretched out his stride and increased his canter to almost a full gallop.

Katlyn was amazed at how quickly the corner of the ring was reached, even at an 'almost gallop'. She slowed Moonbeam down, he was happy to comply. and then walked. She was surprised when she realized how much fun the faster gait turned out to be, particularly when she realized that slowing Moonbeam after the gallop was not going to be a problem.

"That was pretty good," said Warren. "Now that Moonbeam has some idea of what you are asking for, try it again. Keep the same pattern. He may even anticipate it a little this time, which is fine."

By the time Katlyn had asked for the hand gallop several more times, Moonbeam decided this was fun and he entered into the game. He flowed into a full hand gallop.

"One more ingredient," said Warren. "This time, I'm going to gallop just in front of you. Ready?"

"Oh," replied Katlyn, "sure, I guess."

Warren brought his horse in front of Moonbeam, started the canter and at the corner, extended into the hand gallop. Moonbeam perked up his ears at the introduction of a horse in front of him but otherwise continued to listen to Katlyn. Both horses galloped the long side. But Warren continued to gallop, around the corner, through the short end, and down the other long side before he slowed and transitioned to the walk.

Katlyn had not been expecting a lengthy gallop but since Warren had continued to gallop, Moonbeam had continued to follow suit.

Once engaged in the gallop, Katlyn found herself able to relax and enjoy the feeling of the air rushing past her cheeks and the power of Moonbeam's lengthened stride beneath her.

"Not what I was expecting," she said with a big smile," but fun!"

One more thing checked off the undoable list.

Chapter 24

There was one other major hurdle to overcome, however, if she was going to compete in the show. It would require Warren's input and expertise.

After she had washed Moonbeam and put him away, Katlyn went looking for Warren. When she found him, he was about to head to the house for lunch.

"Warren, have you a minute. It's about the show."

"Come to the house, Katlyn I don't think lunch is ready yet. Now, what about the show?"

"Now that it looks like my showing is going to happen, there is one other major problem. In the equitation classes, I might have to change horses. If I might have to ride a strange horse, I'm not sure that I can do that. How will I find out if I'm able to it? Somehow the show ring doesn't seem the right place to discover whether I can or not."

"You are certainly correct that the class isn't the place to find out about riding a strange horse." Warren agreed.

"If I'm right," continued Katlyn, "it is likely that first and second place in the class will be won by Alice and Lucy but that leaves the remaining four ribbons to be won. The only horses I can think of that might be a challenge to ride would be Alice's and Lucy's Morgans. I'm more familiar with Alice's horse since Cilla and I are friends with Alice at the shows. I've been around "Westie", Alice's horse. He is very sensible and laid back for a top winning show horse. Lucy's mare is more of an unknown. I think she is hotter than Westie."

"I don't have an answer for you at this moment, Katlyn. But I'll give it some thought. I know it is solvable, without waiting to test it in the class."

"Thanks, Warren. I know it doesn't have to be resolved today. There is sometime before the show. Looks like Hazel has lunch ready, so I'd better be off. Thanks, again."

Hazel did have Warren's lunch ready, but Katlyn had also spotted Pete walking up the drive from the maintenance shed to meet her for lunch. She couldn't excuse herself from the house fast enough.

Pete was about to enter the barn to look for her when she snuck up behind him and tickled him. He jumped and laughed at the same time. "You didn't know I knew you were ticklish, did you." she giggled. Pete tried to get back at her.

"Won't work." She grinned. "I grew up with two older brothers, remember? I'm immune to tickling."

"You get points for this one, but just wait-you never know," Pete responded.

Hand in hand they went to the rec room. No sooner were they inside with the door closed behind them, then Pete turned Katlyn around and kissed her. "I've missed you." He whispered as he held her close. "Me too," said Katlyn.

"You had to have been in the house to sneak up on me like that," he said. "Anything the matter?"

"No, not really. I had thought of another problem regarding a show class. I wanted to talk to Warren about it."

"I thought you thought the biggest obstacle to showing had been resolved. Now there is another one? How bad a problem?" he asked, flopping on the couch and pulling her down beside him, tucking her under his arm around her shoulders.

"Well, if I'm not in contention for a ribbon in the equitation classes, it's not a problem at all," she explained, nestling comfortably against him. "But if I were to be in the top six under consideration for ribbons, then it would be. You know, don't you, that the top contenders in the class may be asked to ride another exhibitor's horse?"

"No, I didn't know that. I haven't paid much attention to show stuff. But would that be a problem for you?"

"That's the trouble, I don't know. I feel confident now on Moonbeam. I think I'm able to stop thinking about the crash, at least on him. But I don't know if that would be true on a strange horse. What if I had to ride someone else's horse and no matter what he or she looked like or did, it suddenly became Socks to me. I'd be right back where I was before, scared to death and in a panic."

"You're right, that would be a problem" he agreed. "Any thoughts about what to do about it?"

"That's what I was talking to Warren about. He said he would think about it and come up with a plan."

"You could try riding Scout to see how you felt on him," Pet suggested.

"That's a thought. I have never ridden him, so it should be a good test of how I would feel. Would you mind if Warren rode him first? Warren knows my mother's rules so I doubt he would let me get on a strange horse without making sure for himself I would be safe."

"NO, that wouldn't be a problem. Warren is one of the best horsemen I have ever seen. I wouldn't have a worry in the world about him riding Scout."

I'll mention it to Warren. I'm sure he will have some other suggestions about this too. Now, let's eat. I'm starved." Katlyn laughed as she tugged Pete off the couch and headed for the coke machine.

Before he left to go back to work, Pete asked: "Are you going to talk some more with Warren about this today?" If you do, remember my offer." He gave Katlyn a lingering kiss goodbye and left.

When there was a lull later on in the afternoon, Warren called to Katlyn.

"Hazel and I discuss the changing horses situation over lunch. I think we may have come up with something that would work. You have ridden most of the boarder's horses at one time or another but not often enough to truly know them. Let's start with riding each of them again.

"We have a lesson this Saturday, don't we?" Warren asked. Why don't we plan to divide the lesson? Take a half hour to work with Moonbeam, see what exercises he needs to improve and then later maybe in the afternoon, ride Mrs. D's Lightning in the ring for a half hour. He needs the exercise and you can see how you feel about him. How does that sound?"

"Sounds great," said Katlyn, happy to have a plan in place. She added, "when Pete and I were having lunch, he offered to let me ride Scout to test riding a new horse. I told him you might want to ride Scout first and that was fine with him."

That's a good idea. But let's start with horses you are somewhat familiar with first and go from there. Then we'll get to completely new horses."

During the remainder of the week, she often thought about Saturday's plans. She was looking forward to her lesson with Warren with Moonbeam. Now that she was feeling so much more self-confident, she felt she could make some significant progress in Moonbeam's schooling to prepare him for the show.

She was alternately anxious and excited at the thought of riding another horse. *It's been over a month since I have ridden anyone but Moonbeam,* she thought, as various scenarios chased through her mind. *Maybe even thinking about my little blue engine, Thomas, won't work on another horse. But Lightning is such a sweet guy. He takes such good care of Mrs. D. He is like another Moonbeam only smaller. There is no reason on earth to even think that he would do anything wrong. So, what am I worrying about? Then Warren's words clicked in. Challenge your inner voice. It is shouting of feelings, not facts. The fact is you have ridden Lightning before and it was fine. There is no reason to think that now would be any different from before!*

Chapter 25

"You know, Cilla, I almost dread that the show is so close now," Katlyn said. They were lounging in the rec room, finishing their lunch. Katlyn had finished her lesson with Warren, which Cilla had watched. After riding Lightning with Warren, if all went well, they were going on a trail ride.

"What do you mean? I thought you were excited about it. You certainly have been working hard enough to get ready for it." questioned Cilla.

"I know. But there will be so many changes after Labor Day. New school, what's happening with Pete, the show—it's too much. A part of me doesn't want anything to change and at the same time I can't wait for things to get started."

"Wait a minute," interrupted Cilla, "what do you mean "what's happening with Pete". What haven't you told me?"

"He told me Wednesday. I guess with all the decisions and plans about riding strange horses, I forgot to tell you. He was accepted with a late acceptance to Northeastern for the Fall term. He will start the courses he needs for a degree to become a certified something or other, whatever it is that you need to be a greens-keeper at a top golf course. He won't even have to go into the city. He can start out at one of the satellite campuses. And since Northeastern is a co-op school, he can work alternate terms to earn the money for the next term, if he needs to. Between work and school, I don't think I'll get to see him very often. Plus, who knows who he will meet at school. I'm sure there will be lots of new girls to choose from," Katlyn said with a glum look.

"I suppose that might be true, but look at it another way. You will be in high school, with lots of new kids coming from the other junior highs. So, you too will have some new faces to choose among. Ever think of that?

"I can't say that I thought of it like that. But, still…" Katlyn started to say when Cilla added,

"How about your mother's reaction if you went out with a college freshman instead of an ex-caddy from the club? If you 'fudged it' a bit, like maybe you met him through a friend's older brother him or something, wouldn't she be more likely to let you go out with him?

"Cilla, you are a genius! That never occurred to me. All I could think of was how much I was going to miss him. Of course, she said, sobered by reality, he still must want to see me. And it would mean he would have to drive to my place, not that it's all that far, but still."

Laughing, Cilla said, "Katlyn, quit inventing problems! First things first and one at a time We need to get you back to your old 'equestrian queen' self. And then we can worry about the rest of it. Come on, it's time to get Lightning and Peso ready."

As they got the horses ready, Katlyn thought, *whoever named Lightning sure had a sense of humor. Quick, volatile, sudden; he was not. A quieter horse would be hard to find.*

In the ring with Warren, she was pleased to discover she felt relaxed, not at all concerned that the horse was not Moonbeam.

After only ten minutes Katlyn said, "Warren, I don't think Lightning is a very good test subject. I couldn't be afraid on him if I had to. Cilla and I might as well go for our trail ride. I know everything will be fine."

"You needed to find that out, Katlyn," he said. Now you know. Go ahead. Have a good ride."

"The real test," Katlyn said to Cilla as they rode out to the trail, "will be if we canter." She started to laugh. "That is assuming I can get

Lightning into a canter. It's not a gait he is familiar with. I'm not sure Mrs. D ever does anything but walk! But he's very good at that."

However, Lightning was willing to trot and follow Peso along, so they were not confined to just walking. August hadn't released its grip on hot days yet, so the woods were shady and cooler than the open fields. There was the occasional deer fly to contend with but the horses' fly spray kept most of the insects at bay. Cilla was in the lead. For once, not to block Katlyn's horse, but because Lightning wasn't brave enough to be a leader.

Approaching the twin field, Cilla asked "Ready?"

"Go" was the answer from Katlyn. She urged Lightning to pick up a canter, (she had to try very hard to convince him to follow Peso's example). After a few strides of trot, he finally agreed and broke into the canter. Katlyn was so surprised at how rough his canter was, and how hard it was to sit to it, she had no time to think of anything else.

As they walked across the street to pick up the trail into the woods again, Katlyn said, "That was work! What a lousy canter. And he looks as if he is built to have a nice one. Boy, looks can certainly be deceiving."

"Well, were you afraid to canter on him?

"Heck no. It was so hard to sit to his canter, I was concerned I might fall off just because it was so rough. Talk about cement mixers!"

They continued to loop through the trails, picking up whatever gait was suitable for the terrain, eventually arriving back at the barn. Katlyn gave a full report of her success to Warren as they untacked the horses.

Warren only comment on the report was "Did you expect anything other than that?"

"OK, so you knew it would be fine. But you could have said something to me, you know?" Katlyn joked.

"What, and spoil all your fun?" quipped Warren. "Seriously, Katlyn, it was something you had to find out for yourself. No-one can just tell you it will be fine. You must believe in yourself and know deep inside, that it will be fine. Only then, will it be so. As you just discovered."

"I suppose you are right-you usually are! Then who's next on the list?", Katlyn asked.

"How about Red? He's bigger and more powerful, but usually a good boy. Plus, he needs the exercise. How about ten o'clock—ish. I have a lesson before that and they are usually late, but as soon as I am done with her, I'll watch you with Red. Then you and Cilla can go on a trail ride.

"Oh, I almost forgot. Mr. Y will be here tomorrow afternoon. He said about two o'clock. Will you get Alto bridled for him? After he finishes jumping Alto, you might want to hop on him to cool him out. He will be tired and more than ready to just walk or trot a bit. Since he trusts you as he trusts no-one else, I wouldn't anticipate any problems with him, would you?"

"No, I'll admit, when he is jumping, he gets excited but once it is over, he calms down quickly and he is a big baby." Besides, he knows that he doesn't jump when I am on him.

"He will be a good test horse too," she added. "Even though we both know each other well, he still can be a lot of horse to ride sometimes. But I don't think that I will be afraid when I am on him. I've spent so much time getting him to trust me and to let me put a bridle on him without needing a ladder, I know he listens to me."

After helping with some chores around the barn, Cilla and Katlyn were ready to head for home. Cilla's mother was due to pick her up any moment.

She drove in, and as Cilla started toward the car, she said, "Tomorrow will be fun with Red. He is so good on the trails and moves out so willingly. And he is afraid of nothing, so you don't have to worry about him spoking at every little sound or snap of a twig! See you in the morning."

Katlyn gathered her things and headed for the ninth fairway and the pro shop, tired but pleased that the day had gone so well.

Chapter 26

Katlyn lay in bed that night with conflicting thoughts skittering through her mind, delaying her escape into sleep. The thoughts of expanding the list of horses she could ride were exciting. The goal to ride another rider's horse in the equitation classes was becoming more and more attainable. *"Red has big gaits so it feels like he is going faster. I just must keep reminding myself he really isn't. Whenever I have ridden him he has been good about listening to my aids and more importantly, obeying them! I don't think I'll be afraid if he canters. I better not be!*

Alto is another story. I know he trusts me. He follows me as if he was a dog if I don't tie him. But he has had a checkered past. Look how long it took me to get a bridle on him without a battle. And I'm still the only one he will allow to bridle him without a fight. He is still a horse with problems which can erupt at any time. What if he decides to pitch a fit tomorrow with me on him? Granted, he never has, but, there is always a first time. Am I being stupid to even try to ride him? But if I can't ride a horse I have trained for weeks, how will I ever ride a totally strange horse in the show, if I am asked to? Eventually, sleep claimed her.

Tacking up Red on Sunday, Katlyn pushed away her doubts of the night. She concentrated on her upcoming mini-lesson and trail ride. Red was a big, deep chestnut, paint horse. He looked like he might have some draft horse in his pedigree. But then, he needed to be a big, sturdy mount—Mr. D was well over six feet tall with a heavy, muscular build. He wasn't fat, just a big man. He required a big horse to carry him.

Once in the ring, Katlyn put Red through his paces. He behaved as if he knew this ride was somehow special and he had to be on his best behavior. And he was. In no time at all, Warren excused Katlyn and Cilla from the ring and sent them on their way for a trail ride.

When they started the first canter, Katlyn felt herself get tense. Red had such a big canter stride, at first it felt as if he was escaping from something. It took all of Katlyn's will-power to let him continue to canter *Just ride the canter,* she told herself. *It's not fast, he's not running, it's just a big stride!*

With a little help from the little blue engine Thomas, Katlyn was able to relax, sit the canter and begin to enjoy it.

Returning to the barn, Katlyn said to Cilla "One down, one to go." She continued, reassuring herself as much as talking to Cilla. "When he is not jumping, Alto usually is a big baby. And it's not as if this is the first time I have ridden him"

"I don't think you will have any problem with him" Cilla offered. "He is very dependent on you to take care of him. Just remember who is taking care of whom and it will be fine. Besides, thinking about taking care of him will give you something to occupy your mind other than worrying about yourself."

Katlyn had Alto tacked up and ready to go to work before Alto's owner, Mr. Y, arrived. Katlyn knew it was always easier to get Alto to accept someone touching his head when no-one else was around. As she worked around him, getting him ready, Katlyn talked to him which he seemed to enjoy. He swiveled his ears as she moved from one side to the other, listening intently to her.

Katlyn murmured to him, "Alto, you are a very nondescript, very tall, bay horse, all long legs. No wonder you are called Alto. 'Course that is what makes you such a super open jumper, but it would be hard to call you handsome. When you say 'no' to a bridle, it's like trying to bridle a giraffe!" Alto recognized Mr. Y and seemed to like him, but not to the point that he would let him put on the bridle without an argument. He knew if Mr. Y was his rider, that he was going to be jumping which he seemed to like to do. All a rider had to do was point him toward a fence and he was ready, willing and able to jump it.

Mr. Y. arrived at the barn right on schedule. Katlyn and Cilla followed him and Alto to the ring to watch Alto's schooling.

"I jumped him, just once," Katlyn told Cilla as they stood leaning against the newly repaired and freshly painted fence. "It was like riding an elevator. Watch him. He speeds into the jump, seems to almost stop as he sits down to gather himself for the jump, and then springs off his rear to clear it. I like to jump but that once was enough for me. You really must know how to ride that kind of a jump to even stay on."

When Mr. Y. was finished schooling, he brought Alto to the barn. Katlyn had his other saddle ready to switch onto him, for her ride to cool him out. Cilla had Lightning ready to give him some outdoor time and exercise.

"All set, Cilla?" asked Katlyn. Let's walk along the outside hunt course first. Then maybe go out to the trail."

The two horses walking side by side were like Mutt and Jeff-the tall rangy bay and the smaller, stouter paint. But Alto was used to Lightning and happy to have him as his companion. He even shortened his long-legged stride to let Lightning keep up with him.

"Cilla, let's try something," Katlyn said after Alto had cooled down and regained his normal breathing. "As we come across the bottom of the course, by the ninth's tee box, I'm going to start a trot. Then, starting up the hill, I'll ask for a canter, but I'll keep him well to the left-I don't want him to think that we are going to jump the coop or the stone wall at the top. Then I'll bring him to a walk. After cantering up the hill, I hope he will be ready to come to the walk."

"OK. Lightning and I will follow you. Lightning may not think cantering uphill is a great idea, but we'll try."

When Katlyn reached the lower corner of the course, ready to start along the bottom, level part of the course, she asked Alto to trot, keeping well to the inside of the course jumps. At the start of the hill, Katlyn took a deep breath. *We can do this Alto,* she chided herself and asked for a canter. As if to say 'what's the big deal, Katlyn? We do this all the time' Alto broke smoothly into the canter and started up the hill, maybe disappointed that Katlyn kept well to the inside of the jumps, but doing as she asked anyway.

At the top, Katlyn asked for a walk, which Alto willingly gave her. Lightning and Cilla joined them at the top. "We did it" beamed Katlyn. "He was great and I felt fine."

"You two seemed to have a togetherness as you cantered up the slope." complimented Cilla. "In fact, it was a picture of the 'old Katlyn' come back to life that was really nice to see."

Much more used to teasing than compliments from Cilla, Katlyn didn't know what to say in response. After a moment, she acknowledged the compliment with a quiet, "Thank you. I am beginning to feel like the 'old Katlyn', more and more each day." She paused, then added, "But I never could have done it without your help and support. I hope you know that?"

"Yeah, sure, OK. Enough schmaltz for one day. Let's go in. I'm sure we don't have to tell Warren how well it went. His eagle eye is never off your test rides."

A little later, Katlyn approached Warren. "If Pete has time off on Wednesday, and can bring his horse over, do you think it's time to try a totally strange horse? Do you want to ride him first?"

"How do you feel about it? Think you are ready to try it? I don't really need to ride Scout first, but just to be sure, I will. "

"I think that I'm ready. Everything has been going well and I feel much more like my old self. I'm mostly just angry at myself for taking so much time to realize I was the problem. When I get hold of myself and stop harping on what was instead of what' happening right now, I am fine. If I talk to Pete between now and Wednesday, I will let you know if he can make it. If not, we'll just have to see and hope your schedule fits with his. If not on Wednesday, then whenever he has some time available. There is still time before entries close—though come to think of it, not much, is there?"

"No, there isn't. Entries close in two weeks. So, unless you want to take the chance of throwing your money away, making entries you won't ride, you need to be certain that you are up to it. Riding in a class at an "A" rated show is pressure enough. You need all your concentration on riding the requirements of the class —you can't be worrying about anything else."

Monday night Pete called Katlyn. Pete had asked for her number several weeks earlier. Katlyn had been reluctant to give it to him. Not because she didn't want him to have it; she was delighted that he wanted it, but she was concerned about her mother's reaction to Pete calling. She and Pete had finally decided that he would call her at eight o'clock when she was usually in her room if he was able. If she didn't pick up in three rings, he was to hang up. It meant she couldn't talk just then. This Monday. Everything was fine for her to take his call. Katlyn told him about the rides on Red and Alto.

Shyly she asked, "Would you have any time this Wednesday for me to try Scout? Warren and I spoke about it and it's OK with him. He doesn't think he needs to get on Scout first, but he will, just to be sure. Is that OK with you?"

"As I said before, Warren is such a great rider, it'd be great to see him on Scout. As for Wednesday, I have to work at the store in the morning, but I can make it to the barn about two o'clock if that works."

"That would be perfect. I know Warren usually has either trail rides or lessons most mornings but afternoons tend to quiet down, so two-two-thirty-ish should be fine. I'll let him know.

"I know you make it seem so effortless to ride Scout, but I am ready to try it. I'm sure he won't look like he does with you, but that's not really important. So long as I can get on him and concentrate on riding him without panic, that will be enough. I really appreciate it, Pete. See you Wednesday."

Sporting a grin no one else could see, she thought, *What a wonderful, caring guy. I hope he doesn't meet another girl when he is at school! If I can figure out how to get my mother to accept him, then I can officially 'date' him and just maybe, he won't be interested in any of the girls at college. Maybe at the horse show? A friend, a college friend? One who has a horse. Who's father is a professional man-a pharmacist? It might work. If I put Cilla to work on how to do it, it will surely happen!*

Chapter 27

Katlyn was at the barn her usual time on Wednesday. To the side of her that couldn't wait to see Pete again, the morning seemed to drag on forever. *It would be so much nicer if he hadn't had to work and they could have had lunch together, alone, since Cilla couldn't come to the barn on Wednesdays,* she thought. *But, at least I will see him today.*

But then there was the worry about riding Scout. When those thoughts popped up, two o'clock was approaching much too quickly. *What if I panic? What if I am unable to control him?* She was pretty sure *he wouldn't run away with her. But I need to be able to ride him with some semblance of skill and control. I'll be so ashamed if I blow it in front of Pete. He makes it look so easy to ride Scout.*

Finally, Pete rode into the yard. Katlyn was putting a horse away in the back shed and didn't see him arrive. Pete put Scout in an empty stall and went to find Katlyn. He caught up with her before she left the back shed, "There you are" he said. And taking advantage of the privacy afforded them in the back shed, they enjoyed a lingering kiss in greeting before returning to the main barn, hand in hand.

"You ready for your great debut?" he asked.

"Yes and no", answered Katlyn. "Yes, I am anxious to try him. I think that I can do it. No. I will be devastated if I can't. It would mean all the past months' work down the drain!"

"That's not true, Katlyn. Granted, it would be a setback. And entering the show might not be the thing to do. But not that it's the end of everything. All it would mean is that you need to give yourself more time. Besides, I know that you will be able to ride him brilliantly. You'll see. Let's go find Warren."

We located Warren in the house, finishing up a late lunch and short 'relax' break. But he was ready to sit on Scout and then watch me ride (or try to ride) Scout.

Warren swung gracefully onto Scout's saddle and headed for the ring. Scout seemed to know immediately that there was a master aboard. Pete and I watched Warren put Scout through a variety of exercises. Scout was listening intently to every aid Warren gave and performed the exercises flawlessly. It was a real treat to see the skill and grace with which Warren rode a new horse as if they had been together for years.

"You have a beautifully trained horse, Pete. Did you train him yourself?"

"Yes, I bought him when he was just green-broke at three and a half and have had him ever since. He is very smart, sometimes too smart. There have been times when I have been pushed to figure a way to outsmart him to get him to learn to do something my way rather than what he thought was the right way."

"Well, there certainly is no problem with Katlyn getting on him. He is a real gentleman," said Warren. "OK, Katlyn, he's all yours."

I had been so mesmerized watching Warren's beautiful ride, I had forgotten that it would be my turn in a few minutes. With Warren's words, all my doubts came screaming for attention again. As Pete and I left the rail to go to Scout, Pete gave me a quick squeeze around the shoulder and said: "Just talk to Scout and tell him how wonderful and smart he is and he will do anything for you."

With Pete there, Scout stood as still as a statue while I mounted him. *That's a good start,* I thought, as I asked him to take the track of the ring. Scout was a good-sized horse with a lot of thoroughbred breeding behind him as well as some paint breeding. He responded eagerly, settling into a big swinging walk. The old negativity started to surface. A voice warned 'he is getting ready to go-to leave'. *Think of Thomas, I told myself. Scout isn't doing anything but his normal big, forward walk. Listen to your muscle memory. Let your back relax and become one with him.*

After a half-dozen strides, I (and Thomas) conquered that negative voice. I made my back relax and join in the rhythm of the walk. It was a very comfortable, forward walk with no tension in it. It was nearly impossible to maintain a stiffness and not flow with him.

I started to think about the patterns I would have to perform in the equitation class. Could I perform them on Scout? "Only one way to find out," I told myself. "Scout, you are a handsome boy," I said, "let's trot a nice working trot and then make a perfect round circle." Scout flicked his ears as if to acknowledge the request and smoothly picked up the trot. Remembering that I might need to help him bend through his middle with my outside leg, he responded to the aid and executed the circle perfectly.

Now the big test-the canter, I thought. I knew in order to be given any consideration in the class, it had to be immediately upon request, from the walk directly into the canter with no trot steps and smoothly into an easy, controlled canter. I could perform it on Moonbeam. *Could I manage it on Scout?* I asked myself.

"OK, Scout. Let's do it." I brought him to the walk, asked for his attention. "Scout, get ready, a new gait." I put my seat bone down, lifted and as if to say 'what's the big deal?' Scout smoothly lifted into a lovely canter on the correct lead. It was impossible to do anything but enjoy the moment. A big grin was on my face as we cantered the ring. In a moment of foolishness, I even threw away the reins as Scout continued to maintain a steady canter. Just a voice command brought him to the walk. I leaned over, hugged him and told him what a wonderful boy he was. I turned to Pete; "What did you ever do to deserve such a wonderful horse?" I teased.

"I would say that you passed that test with flying colors, Katlyn," Warren said. "And remember, if you have to change horses, it will likely be with Alice or Lucy. Both of those horses are well trained and know their job. Any other horse will be much more like schooling Moonbeam, so just ride it like that."

I was glad that Pete didn't have to leave right away. I was still wound up like the proverbial eight-day clock. So many of my hopes and dreams seemed to fall into place with that ride. I could now make my entries for the show, sure that if I had to change horses, I could manage it. It might take a lot of concentration and a little help from 'Thomas', but I could do it.

We put Scout in a stall, gave him some hay, and went to the rec room for a coke.

"Come sit down," asked Pete, indicating beside him on the couch.As I sat down he put his arm around my shoulder. "That's better. Now a couple of deep breaths and relax."

It felt so good tucked into him I had no trouble relaxing. "I did it, didn't I?" I murmured, still astounded that I had.

"You certainly did-in spades."

"I think that ride was the final push I needed to really convince myself that I could stop re-living that awful ride and ride the way I knew I could. Thank you for that-you and Scout." I turned and accentuated the thank-you with a heartfelt kiss.

Chapter 28

I was quiet as Cilla, Pete and I readied Moonbeam for the equitation class. I was reviewing the patterns we would have to perform but was often interrupted by thoughts of being asked to ride another competitors horse.

"Katlyn, stop thinking about riding another horse! I know that's what you are doing," scolded Cilla.

Pete joined in, "Think about how well you rode Scout. You didn't know him at all, yet rode him perfectly. You can do that with any horse that is in this class. As you said before, the only ones who might be a challenge would be Alice's and Lucy's Morgans. But you can handle either one of them. I know you can."

With that encouragement, I mounted and rode to the warm-up ring. Most of the others in the class were also warming up so not only did I warm-up Moonbeam, but I had a chance to watch the other competitors and observe how they rode their horses.

It wasn't a huge class so there was room to enter the ring and space ourselves without being right on the tail of another's horse. The major challenge of the class was the figure eight at the canter with the simple change of lead. Moonbeam remembered his schooling and did it smoothly and correctly.

The ringmaster called for a walk. While the class walked, the judges conferred. This was the strategic point. If there were clear winners, we would be asked to line up and the ribbons would be awarded. If they were undecided, the ones they were still uncertain about, would be asked to come to the center to change horses.

"Moonbeam, this is it, I whispered. If someone else rides you, you can be as bad as you want. But don't worry, you are still my favorite boy." I had no sooner said this than the ring steward called our number to come to the center of the ring. I looked to see who else had been called. Several other numbers had also been called so it was still uncertain who was being asked to ride which horse.

Everyone dismounted and the steward told each rider what horse he/she was to ride. As I had thought (and hoped), I was to ride Lucy's Morgan. Alice was not among those asked to change which I took to mean she most likely had been determined to be in first place. Only the other five ribbons were undecided. The steward gave everyone a leg up into the saddle and told us we had a few minutes to aquaint ourselves with the horse before we would be judged. He would announce when judging was resumed.

I took a deep breath—in fact several— while I talked to Lucy's mare. I started her on a very light contact rein and gradually took up the contact. *OK. So far so good,* I thought. Checking that no-one was immediately behind me, I said to the mare, "Well, mare, have you brakes?" The answer was a resounding 'yes', very good ones. We resumed the walk just as the steward announced judging would begin again.

After observing the riders on the new horses at the walk, we were asked for the trot. I didcovered, as I had suspected, Lucy's mare took only the slightest whisper of an aid to respond. Lucy would be finding Moonbeam very different!

It took severeal strides for me to adjust to the mare's shorter trot stride but then I was in rhythym with her. I was so busy concentrating on the challenge of figuring her out, how to get a smooth ride and transitions, I had no time to worry about the fact that I was riding a strange horse. She was a fun horse to ride, different but not scary. I knew she was trying to figure me out as well and trying her best to do as I asked, even when how I asked was different from what she was used to.

The first transition into canter was not immediate but when she did pick it up, it was on the correct lead and controlled. Fortunately, the judges asked for two transitions into canter before we had to do the figure eight. By then, I had mostly figured her out, I thought.

OK, girl. Here we go for the big push, I thought as we took our turn to execute the figure eight pattern. This time the mare picked up the canter immediately and we started the first part of the figure. The simple change transition to the steps of trot could have been smoother, but at least she picked up the canter again right away. As we completed the second half, I gave her a pat and transistioned nicely into the trot and then walk. I walked the mare to the center of the ring with the other riders while the final few riders completed their figure eight patterns. We all dismounted, mounted our own horse and went to the rail at a walk while the judges conferred and made their final decision.

After several minutes we were asked to line-up again in the center with all the exhxibitors of the class. The steward called out a number, starting with sixth place. Not me, but there were other horses in the line. Not fifth, not fourth. Then I heard my number. As I moved forward to received my ribbon, I was still in shock-I had placed third! Right behind Lucy in second and Alice in first. I could hardly believe it. As the winners took a victory lap around the ring, Moonbean seemed to realize how wonderful it was and I had to hold him back at the canter-he was ready to hand gallop!

Pete and Cilla met me as soon as I was out of the ring, all smiles and congratulations. I knew Pete wanted to give me a big hug and I wanted it just as much, but knowing my mother was waiting for me to come to her after the class, I stayed on Moonbean and rode him up to the barn. I hoped that in the privacy of Moonbeams stall, I wowuld be properly congratulated by Pete. And I was. Cilla volunteered to take Moonbeam's saddle to the tack room, giving Pete and I a moment alone.

With Moonbeam washed and settled until later that afternoon, the big mmoment had come—time to introduce Pete to Mom. Cilla, Pete and I with cold cokes in our hands, walked over to where Mom had been watching the class.

"Mom, you know Cilla, and this is George Peterson, a friend of ours. He has his own horse so we sometimes trail ride together. He is starting college next week." I held my breath awaiting my mother's reaction. To my surprise, there was no reaction, just a cordial, "Nice to meet you, George."

"Ah, everyone calls him Pete, Mom," I said.

"Nice to meet you, Mrs. Lange. Wasn't Katlyn win great? She is such a natural rider." offered Pete.

"Mom, Pete is going to join us for lunch, then he has to leave for work. He can't stay to watch the real fun class with the five-gaited horses."

"Katlyn, you know I don't know much about horse shows, so were you pleased with your rides?" asked Mrs. Lange.

Before I could answer, Cilla chimed in "Mrs. Lange, for Katlyn to get a third in that equitation class was spectacular. Alice and Lucy are the top two equtation riders in New England. For Katlyn to get switched onto Lucy's mare and ride her so well is outstanding! It's a really big feather in her cap. Just ask Warren. He's so pround of her his grin doesn't stretch big enough."

Laughing at Cilla enthusiasm and praise I said, "Cilla cut it out. But yes, Mom, I am really pleased" To myself, I added *and I made a comeback-I conquored my fears and proved I can ride again as I used to.*

Turning to Pete, Mon asked," Where are you going to college, Pete?"

"I start my classes at Northeastern next week. I plan to major in land management/environmental studies."

"Do you live around here?" Mom asked.

"Yes, I live in Salem, just over the Peabody line. My father is a pharmacist and owns the pharmacy in the square," Pete said.

"Hey, enough of this. Let's eat," I said."I'm starved." I went to our car and retrieved the picnic basket from the back of the car. We spred a blanket for us to sit on, Mom had her folding chair. Introductions sucessfully accomplished, we ate and chit-chated until Pete had to leave.

While we were eating, Mrs. Pierson came over to join us. I hadn't expected her to be at the show, so I was surprised to see her.

"Marge, she said, "you must be very proud of Katlyn. She did a beautiful job with Moonbean in both classes. I hardly recognized my own horse. Congratulations, Katlyn, you rode Moonbeam to perfection."

As she was speaking, I got up to get the ribbons Moonbeam had won. I handed them to Mrs. P. "As the owner of the horse," I said, " these belong to you. I can't thank you enough for letting me show him."

"Oh my goodness, Katlyn. I wouldn't dream of taking them. You earned them so you should have them. I appreciate the thought, but no, they are yours.

"Thank you so much, Mrs. Pierson. Moonbeam is a wonderful horse. I had such a good time schooling him and he is so smart it wasn't work at all."

We finished eating and packed up the picnic things. It was almost time for Pete to leave when Warren came by. He stopped and gave me a big hug as he said to Mom, "Katlyn did herself pround today, Mrs. Lange. It's no small feat to get changed onto the horse of one of the two top equitation riders, ride her as well as Katlyn did and place in the ribblons just after these top riders. That showed real skill and commitment. I can't tell you how proud of her I am."

I blushed in embarrassment at his praise. I knew that he wasn't speaking of just the show rides. He was also referring to my success in the battle to put that disasterous ride behind me.

"I must run. As you can imaging, I have a million things to do but I wanted to be sure to congratulate you, Katlyn, while I had a moment."

As Warren left, Pete said,"I must be on my way also, Katlyn. Sorry I can't stay for your final class, but I know you will ace it as you did the first two. I'll call you if I may to find out how you did?"

Out of the corner of my eye, I watched for my mother's reaction to this offer. Seeing no negative reaction, I answered, "sure, that would be great. It's too bad you have to miss the five gaited class, though. There isn't anything like being there when this particular ring steward calls out in that special voice of his 'Ra-a-ack O-o-on'. Only he seems to be able to draw out the words so that horses and spectators join in the excitement and fun and the horses explode into the rack while the spectators hoot and holler. It's no wonder he is the chief ring steward at the Madison Square Garden show in New York. He is the only one to call out the gaits for the five-gaited classes there.

I'll walk with you to your car. I'll be right back Mom. It's almost time for the five-gaited class."

"That went well, I think," I said to Pete. "Mom didn't seem to think anything of it. One of the big school things in mid-October is the all-school Harvest Fling. If I had her permission to ask you to be my date for it, would you come?"

"Are you kidding? Of course, I would come. It would be fun. Do you think your mom will say yes?"

"I'm not sure, but I think so. It's a major school event. If we double date with one of my friends, like Patty who lives next door it isn't as if we would be alone on a date."

"Well, think about it. In the meantime, ride well this afternoon and I'll talk to you tonight. And congratulations again for super riding."

It always left such an empty spot somewhere deep inside me whenever he left, I delayed returning to Mom. I readied the excuse that I had to check on Moonbeam while I regained my composure. I wasn't ready yet to allow Mom to see how much Pete meant to me.

Cilla, Mom and I watched the five-gaited class, with all its fanfare and fun. Then it was time to get Moonbeam organized for the final class of the day, the bridle path class. This was a rather low key class, without most of the fancy horses that entered in road hack. Moonbeam and I had a chance at winning it.

As Moonie and I entered the ring I glanced at the 'fateful corner'. With its fresh coat of paint, it was indistinguishable from the rest of the fencing.And I thought, *now I can finally say it is also 'indistinguishable' in my mind. It happened, it's over and it's gone! Thank Goodness!*

With that thought, I whispered to Moonie, "let's ride this last class for fun. Show them what a real bridle path horse looks like." Moonbeam seemed to understand or maybe it was because I was totally relaxed, but whichever the reason, he was a superstar. We just couldn't do anything wrong. As a result, we added a blue ribbon to complete our collection for the day.

By the time I had cleaned the tack, cleaned Moonbeam, and settled him for the night, I was more than ready to call it a day and head for home. I was tired but it had been a great show. Tomorrow was another day for the show but I had not entered any classes. I had road hack and bridle path classes on Labor day, the third day of the show, but they were well spaced apart so it was no effort to get ready for each class.

I asked Mom "how did you like the show?" since it was her first time at one of the big circuit shows.

"It was very interesting I hadn't realized how many of the club members had horses they showed or had someone show for them." She paused. "I also hadn't realized how well-thought-of you were. There were a number of people who stopped by to say hello and tell me what a talented rider my daughter was. They were most complimentary. And, if I didn't say it before, let me say it now, congratulations for a successful day!"

"Thanks, Mom." was all I could say.

A companionable silence ensued during the remainder of the drive home.

Marge Lange's thoughts, however, were anything but silent. *To think that I almost lost this by my arrogance and lack of understanding. Jerry was right, nothing would have made up for her having nothing to do with me. I still need to guide her, but I also need to realize she is who she is, not who I think she ought to be. It won't always be easy—she is so different from me!—but I have to try. And I will because I love my daughter, no matter who she is or turns out to be.*

The End

www.ingramcontent.com/pod-product-compliance
Lightning Source LLC
Chambersburg PA
CBHW060641130626
46555CB00002B/909